Love, Lies 'N Betrayal

"There's always warning before destruction!"

Courtney Simone

Love, Lies 'N Betrayal

Published by Dream Ink Publications

ISBN 978-1-7338530-0-2

"Loyalty isn't defined by how long you've known a person, but by the love they show, the things they will do for you and will not do to you."

- Courtney Simone

Table of Contents

Chapter 1

"Good Girl Gone Bad"

I'm Tara. A chill chick who tries to stay away from drama and focuses on my hustle and success. I don't hang with too many bitches, but I have two best friends I would go to war for; one of them being Chanel. Chanel and I met in middle school. At one point, we hated each other, all over a stupid-ass dude neither one of us took seriously. We were both dealing with him at the same time and started beefing. I was never the kid in school anyone had to worry about. I was cool with everybody, minded my own business and made straight A's; but Chanel, on the other hand, was the total opposite. She was a damn bully, and of course, she tried me. Yeah, we fought over our boyfriend, but after that, we both ended up dropping the dude and Chanel and I got to really know each other. We started hanging out and I realized she was a cool-ass chick. We clicked and have been cool ever since.

Chanel lived a different lifestyle than I did. She was a badass! She fought a lot, skipped school, smoked weed and barely made passing grades. Her mom was a single parent, they lived in the hood and struggled to make ends meet. Her mom worked two jobs and was hardly ever home. Chanel wasn't the only child, though. She has a fine-ass brother named Norris.

1

He was the finest nigga I had ever laid my eyes on. He was a senior when I was a freshman. Norris was three years older than I was, but for some reason, I had a thing for older guys. Not like the older the wiser, because all men are stupid as hell.

Anyways, Norris stood 6'1", and had light, golden-brown, smooth skin with hazel eyes and a toned body. He was a very popular and athletic kid who played football, basketball and ran track. Almost every girl at Seabrook High wanted him. Girls threw themselves at him left and right. If one girl wasn't all over him, there was another that was.

I had the biggest crush on him myself. I was always over at their house. I had my eyes on him for a while, but believe it or not, I was always too shy to speak to him. He acknowledged me, but never showed he was interested. That didn't change how I felt about him, though.

I always thought he was out of my league. There were so many other girls in school and in the neighborhood that were on his age level, were prettier than I was, and had bigger breasts and booty than I did. I always told myself he would never want me. Well, at least that's what I thought, until one day over at their house changed my life forever.

That day went a little something like this… Chanel and I sat on the porch, one, hot Saturday. Bored out of our damn minds, we decided to chill and watch Norris and his friends hoop, as we gossiped about shit that had nothing to do with us. While Chanel talked the majority of the time, I had my eyes on Norris. He was shirtless, with gym shorts on, showing off his muscular arms and perfectly-formed six-pack. His fine-ass body was dripping sweat, as it glistened in the sun like diamonds on a rich bitch's hand.

Looking like an NBA star, making endless shots, I lusted over him. I wasn't paying attention to shit Chanel was talking about. Norris perfected everything he did, and he always looked good while doing it.

2

Just watching him hoop with his boys, as if he was a pro, turned me on. Hell, as a young virgin, almost anything turned me on, back then. Damn! He was the shit back then. He had me close to fainting on Chanel's porch that day. As I drooled over him, not taking my eyes off him for one second, I sat there thinking about everything I wanted to do to him. From that moment on, I knew he had to be mine.

That night when they finished playing ball, we all went in the house and chilled in the living room. Norris left us and went straight to the shower. I wanted to follow him badly, but I sat my thirsty-ass right on the couch with everybody else. I knew he was used to girls throwing pussy at him, but I wanted to play with his mind a little bit, show him something different, make him put in work and play hard to get.

Let me just say, although I was a virgin at the time, I didn't mind getting fucked by his fine-ass. I always wondered what sex felt like, how it would be the day I lost my virginity and who I would lose it to. I kept calm, though, and chilled on the couch, as if I didn't have these nasty-ass thoughts running through my head.

About 20 minutes later, I went in the kitchen to get some ice for my soda, and guess who walked in the kitchen, asking me if I would fix him some as well… Yep, fine-ass Norris. I damn sure wasn't an ice cube, but my ass almost melted!

I was shocked he was finally saying more than just hi and bye. I didn't know what to say. My heart was pounding in my chest! Although I liked him, there was no way in hell I was going to show him that. I definitely had plans on playing hard to get. I stuck to the plan and that's exactly what I did.

I replied and said, "Hell naw, fool, but I'll leave it here for you to do it yourself."

I grabbed my glass off the counter and walked out the kitchen, leaving him standing there. When I looked back to wink at him, he was still staring at me, smiling from ear to ear, with those perfectly-whitened teeth that sat between his soft, juicy, dark pink lips (Ok, no I had never felt his lips to actually know if they were soft or not, but it damn sure looked as if they were). I gave him a smirk back and went to sit back on the couch next to Chanel, as if nothing happened.

I did whisper in her ear, "Girl, yo' brother diggin' me. He better keep still before he gets cuffed."

She laughed and said, "I'm definitely hooking y'all up! You're lucky you're my girl now." We both giggled and sipped our sodas like it was some Henny and cranberry on ice.

The night started winding down and everybody had already left. Running my mouth and wanting to be up in a nigga face left me with no way home and no luck on getting in touch with my sister, mom or dad.

Norris had a car and a license, and he was willing to take me. I didn't know if he was just being generous or had a game of his own he was playing. I wanted him but wasn't sure if I was really ready (Yeah, I played hard in the kitchen, but it was all a front). I would be nervous as hell to be in the car alone with him. I knew Chanel really well. I knew for sure she wasn't riding and, sure enough, she didn't.

The entire ride I looked out the window and was quiet until Norris called me out about it.

"What you so quiet for? Huh, Gorgeous," he asked.

I smirked, looked at him and said, "What's there to talk about?"

"Well, you can start by telling me about yourself."

"You know almost everything."

"I don't know everything. Tell me this, boss lady. Why you so mean?"

(Sucking my teeth) "I am not mean," I told him, as I chuckled a little bit, while rolling my eyes.

"Why you couldn't fix my drink?"

"Why should I? You ain't my dude!"

"Damn, so it's like that," Norris asked, laughing.

"Yup, it's like that," I said back.

"I like you," Norris said, as he shocked the hell out of me. The conversation was getting deep, making me more nervous than what I was. It had me hoping to come up to my house soon.

"What you mean?"

"You cool, man! I wanna get to know you!"

"Ha! Is that right?" Man, when he said that, my heart started pounding! That was the moment I dreamt about. I was still in denial that it was actually happening, though. Still sticking to my plan, I never showed any signs of how much he excited me.

Thankfully, we were pulling up at the house and I was getting ready to hop out, until he stopped me.

"Can I get yo' number," he asked.

"Maybe one day, just not this one! Thanks for the ride, though," I yelled, as I slammed the car door.

"Damn," I heard Norris whisper.

Yeah, he was diggin' me more than I thought. Weeks went by of us seeing each other in school and at his house. We flirted and played around with each other from time to time, but I was still brushing him off slightly. Then, one day, I finally decided to give Norris my number.

He called me the next day, but I didn't answer. He called me a few days more, before I decided to pick up. After that day, I decided to answer, we talked and hung out. We talked for about a month and a half, before making it official on Valentine's Day. He bought me roses, candy, a huge teddy bear and a card that asked if I would be his girl. We started talking more, hanging out more, and then went on our first, official date a month after that.

It wasn't nothing major. Norris didn't have much money. He worked part-time at Foot Locker, and at that time, it was cool. We were still young; and I didn't expect anything extravagant. He was perfect to me. He didn't have to shower me with money or gifts to win my heart… that was already a done deal. Besides, I was a spoiled bitch. Anything I wanted that Norris could possibly buy, I already had or could get from my parents.

We wanted dinner and ended up at Applebee's. I liked Applebee's, so I didn't trip. We talked, laughed and smiled the majority of the time. You know how that immature love is. I was still nervous around him and a little shy too. I couldn't eat like I wanted to, and I didn't say much. It was nice, though. Not only was he fine, he was also a gentleman as well.

Opening and closing doors for me, allowing me to walk in before him, he checked on me multiple times in the night; yeah, all that. He treated me like royalty. That was my first, real relationship, so I wasn't knowledgeable about what it should be like, I only knew what I saw and thought I wanted. I had a crush on him for the longest time and we had the best times together. It all felt so real!

On the way back to his spot, he told me how much he enjoyed the night with me and how much he appreciated the opportunity he was given to date me. He was so charming. I idolized him. Nothing he did was wrong, in my eyes, even if it was. I could literally see this guy commit murder and believe he didn't do it. I truly thought he was heaven-sent. Everything with Norris, so far, was all that I'd hoped it to be.

When we got to his house, we went in his room, laid across the bed and watched Cops. He loved that show. I didn't give a fuck about it, but because he liked it, I loved it. He cuddled with me, held me in his arms tightly, as we watched TV. He whispered in my ears, told me he never wanted to let me go and that he loved me.

For him, I was head over heels, so I said it back. I really meant it too. Well, at least I thought I did. I knew it was still early and I probably didn't know what love meant at such a young age, but I was now dating my crush. Who really gave a fuck? (We have all been there and done that, so don't look at me crazy).

He grabbed my face, placed the tip of his nose on mine, looked me directly in my eyes and started kissing me with those wet, soft lips (They actually were softer than I thought). I closed my eyes, as we tongue kissed and sucked on each other's lips. I was getting into it. Not thinking about what it all could lead to.

His hands moved from my jaws to my neck. He held my neck tight, rubbed on my shoulders and chest, as his hands moved down to my breasts. He put his hands in my bra, rubbed my nipples, and as his hands moved down, I could feel his dick getting harder and harder on my legs. Norris grabbed my hand with one of his and placed it on his dick; with the other hand, he went into my panties and rubbed my pussy. The more he kissed me and rubbed my pussy, the wetter I got, and within seconds my shit was dripping. I was young, but I was ready. This pussy was no joke and I knew that any nigga that got in this would never be able to leave me alone.

He moved his lips to my nipples and sucked all over them. At that point, I didn't know where my head was. I was in a different place, mentally. I was a virgin, I couldn't tell you what I was thinking. My mind went blank. It felt so good. I had never felt that feeling before. My mind was racing in so many different directions.

I grabbed on him. I gripped it really tight, and that's when I realized it was enormous! I had never touched him, even though we chilled together many, many times. He was much larger than

I'd ever thought it would be. *No way that was normal*, I thought to myself. Brah was working with a monster.

As I grabbed it, all I could think about was how it would feel inside me. As we continued to get affectionate, his dick got harder. I wanted to shove it in me, I was that curious. He ended up getting on top of me, pulled my dress up, my panties down and went from sucking my nipples to slurping my pussy. I mean, he slobbered all over that shit.

His soft lips suffocated my clit. I moaned and moaned! That was my first time getting oral and damn sure wasn't going to be my last. He was so good at it! Like I said before, he perfected everything he did, and that was no different. He knew what he was doing. He made me feel so good. I didn't think I could take it. As I started wiggling, he held me tighter.

"Where you going, baby," he asked.

I couldn't speak. I mumbled some crazy shit I can't recall.

He reached in his pocket to grab a condom, opened it and rolled it on. He got up, put it in a little and I immediately started moaning. Biggest mistake I think I had made that far in my life was fucking something so big for the first time.

"Are you ok, baby," he asked.

"I'm...I'm a virgin," I said, warily.

"Oh yeah? Is that right? I'll take care of you, I'll be easy," he said.

He eased it in more and more. As he penetrated me, I got louder. We went for about 20 minutes. I knew for sure I loved him after that! There were no doubts about it.

When it was over, he kissed me on my cheek and told me how amazing it was. When Norris went to the bathroom, I laid across the bed in a daze. I looked at the ceiling, with so many emotions. I couldn't believe we fucked! I was still shocked that I actually lost my virginity. I didn't know how I should have felt, but I must admit it, he impressed me. He made losing my virginity worth waiting for.

I could tell he was experienced. I didn't know if that was a good thing or a bad thing, but I knew what we did was breathtaking, and it couldn't stop there! He was so much better in bed than I thought he would be. I was only 14 years old and he was 17 (Yeah, I know, such a young slut, right? I was moving too fast)! My mom had no idea we were dealing with each other, but if she ever found out I was no longer a virgin, all hell would break lose.

Chapter 2

"Lies and Manipulation"

The first year of our relationship was smooth. Once he graduated from Seabrook High, he went off to college on a football scholarship. His college was three hours away. He was so damn far, I hated it! I held up well, though. I hardly saw him, but I stayed faithful.

After a year of him being away, things seemed to get rocky between us. There we were, two and a half years in our relationship. I was a junior in high school, dating a college sophomore. I knew once he went off, shit would change. I couldn't compare to all those fine-ass college girls he was around on the daily. I knew deep down that we probably wouldn't last, but Norris meant everything to me, so I was willing to try as long as I needed to.

As time went on, things got worse. A few weeks later, we had summer break, so I decided to pop up on Norris and stay a few days with him. Chanel came along to spend some time with Norris too, and of course to find her a fine-ass college nigga.

Michelle took us both up there (Michelle is my oldest and only sister. She is four years older than I am and a total bitch). Chanel went to knock on the door, while I was still in the car, talking to Michelle. Norris answered the door, timorously, with a towel around his waist.

"What... What, are you doing here, Chanel," he stuttered, in a shaky voice.

"Hey, brother, I missed you! Just got out the shower," Chanel asked, as she bogarted her way through the door.

"NO! I have company! Whatever you do, do not tell Tara. Please, sis, I'm begging you," Norris whispered.

"COMPANY?! Norris, why? How am I not supposed to tell my best friend my brother, who supposedly loves her, is cheating on her? How? Don't put me in the middle of that. In other words, I don't know shit, since I can't take a side," Chanel whispered.

Guess what? It was too late. I walked in the door, saw Norris in a towel and overheard the last sentence Chanel said. Viscously, I went through his apartment like a dog, looking for a piece of meat. I tore his shit up and didn't give one fuck about it! I was turning things over, slamming doors, checking in the kitchen, checking in the shower, nobody was there. I paced back and forth from the kitchen to the living room, as I tried calming myself. Then, I decided to walk in the bedroom. There she was… terrified. She was rushing to put on her clothes and shoes, but I stopped the bitch in her tracks!

"Who the fuck is you and why the fuck is you naked in my man's bedroom," I asked. She never spoke!

"Huh, bitch," I continued. Chanel and Norris came running in the room.

"Is this your bitch, Norris? Huh? Is this what you do out here when I'm back at home being faithful to your nasty-ass? Is it," I asked Norris, fiercely.

"No, baby, no, please calm down. I'm sorry, she's a nobody," Norris wept.

"A nobody," the mysterious girl repeated, as she ran past Norris out the apartment.

"Yes, bitch, a nobody," I hollered back at her, as my voice echoed in his apartment!

I stormed out, as Michelle walked in. Chanel ran after me, yelling, "Tara, wait!"

"What the hell is going on right now," Michelle asked, sternly.

"Tara, baby, wait," Norris yelled.

As Norris sat on the floor, with his back against the door and hands on his head, we drove off.

Nothing went as planned. My heart was broken into pieces. The guy I loved, had been committed to for the past two and a half years, the first and only guy I gave myself to, lied and cheated on me. Somehow, I ended up blaming myself for the hurt and pain that he caused me. I had so many questions about why he would want to do that to me. Why me, out of all people?

All I did was love him, honor him, respect him! I wanted to build a future with him. He wasn't just anybody, he was my everything, and I thought I was his everything, but maybe I wasn't good enough for him. I couldn't have been good enough if he wanted someone else. My mind was filled with questions and thoughts, my eyes were filled with tears, and my heart was filled with pain. I asked myself why, over and over.

Chanel comforted me, as Michelle did the opposite.

"I've been telling you time and time again he is no good! He is a known ho, Tara. Everybody knew that! Girls in my college talk about him and how they have dealt with him! Leave him alone," Michelle fussed.

It felt like I was in the car with my mom, with all the preaching she did. Why would I take advice from somebody who couldn't even keep a man? I never said that out loud, though, because that argument would have never ended; and besides, I had enough to deal with. The time I needed my sister the most, she was being unsupportive; as usual, though. I think she hated me since I was born. She was one of those spoiled-ass, rich kids who wanted to be the only child.

Although that explained why our relationship was falling apart, nothing made sense. I wanted to call him so badly, but I knew I needed to calm down first. I always played innocent, but deep down inside, I could be a vicious bitch if I needed to. I wanted him to explain to me why he had cheated, but I wasn't ready to listen. I wanted to just give up and move on, but I was still deeply in love with him.

I didn't understand how it was possible to love the person that hurt me so badly. I wanted nobody but Norris. I didn't want to start over. Love was like a gamble; putting your all into it, hoping for the best outcome, but possibly getting the worst. Knowing that I could potentially end up with someone worse than Norris, I was willing to hear him out.

He called me every day. It seemed like he called a million times a day, but I still didn't answer. I stayed at home and laid in the bed for days, alone, down and depressed. After about six days of rejecting him, I finally answered.

"Hello!"

"Hey, baby… Tara, you there?"

"What, Norris?"

"I understand your upset, baby, and you have every right to be. I made a careless mistake. I fucked up badly, but I can't lose you. I can't, baby. I don't know what I would do without you."

"Did you fuck her, Norris?"

"No, baby, I didn't. I promise. Chanel knocked at the door before it happened."

At that point, I was just relieved. There was no way I could share that good loving with another bitch.

"I really can't believe you would do this to me. I did nothing but love you. I was faithful to you. I gave you all of me, literally. My first love, you took my virginity, you were all I knew; but there you were, doing you, not giving a fuck about us, what we had, what we could have been," I told Norris, as I cried heavily.

"Baby, please! I hate to hear you cry. I'm sorry. I really am. I can't…"

"You are very sorry, Norris. You are absolutely right. And the last thing I want is a sorry nigga on my side. I can't do this anymore, Norris!"

"Baby? Baby, I love you. Do you love me?"

"Of course, I do!"

"Will you give me a second chance? I wanna make it up to you."

"I don't know!"

"OK, baby, I'll give you some time to think. I just got in my class, so I'll call you later. I love you! I love you with all my heart, beautiful!"

"…I love you too!"

"Talk to you soon, baby, bye." Then, we both hung up.

After that, Norris called me every day. When I came home from school a couple days later, I instantly noticed pretty, bright, red roses sitting on the dining room table. I love flowers. Smelling them was so refreshing and calming, just what I needed. I walked over to them, leaned in to get a whiff and a card nipped my nose. I grabbed the card, realizing my name was on the front. I opened up the card and pulled out the note. The note read, "I love you, miss you and can't wait to see you. Love, your future husband." I had lots of balloons as well. He was really putting in work to win me back. Although I was flattered, there was no way I could give in that easy. Especially, not over some cheap-ass flowers and cheesy-ass lines.

After playing hard to get for about three weeks, we sat down, talked about everything and I took him back. I couldn't resist, I loved him! Besides, he didn't fuck the girl, and everybody deserves a second chance, right? After getting back together, our relationship was ok, but he didn't waste any time fucking up again.

Chapter 3
"The Trap"

We went strong for about four months and then I found out he was texting and calling other chicks. Not only that, I found a sex video in his phone that he recorded himself! I was furious! I was devastated! That really blew me away. It was disrespect on another level. I was done - for good. It was time I moved on.

His cheating, his lies, the manipulation. He was a really attractive guy. Not saying that was a pass, but it was expected. I told him I just couldn't deal with the cheating, it was unacceptable; especially, when it was being done to a faithful woman who loved him. We would always be friends, but I couldn't see myself being more than that.

It hurt so much to make that decision. It took everything in me to be able to deliver those words to him, but I knew I didn't deserve what he had done to me and how I was being treated! Yeah, I loved him unconditionally, but I was also a strong, young woman and I refused to degrade myself for anyone! I was raised better than that! I knew I deserved so much better, and at the right time, I would get just that.

When Michelle found out, all she did was talk shit.

"About time! About time," she said to me.

"You don't need him anyways! He don't have shit! I don't know why you wanted him in the first place," she continued, rolling her eyes and frowning almost the entire time she talked.

A couple weeks went by. I was doing pretty damn good, to say I was dealing with a difficult breakup. Seemed like guys were all over me more at school, as if they knew what happened between Norris and me. I felt like I was the shit!

I was doing me, feeling great; then, while I was at school one day, I started feeling nauseous all of a sudden. I felt very faint and my vision got blurry. Chanel rushed me to the nurse's office, where she checked me out and asked me questions. Before I knew it, I was on the floor.

I heard loud voices around me but can't recall what was said or whose voices they were. I woke up in the hospital with my mom, Michelle, Chanel and her mom next to me. I was so confused.

"What happened," I asked, in a frightened voice.

Mom stood up next to me and rubbed my hair.

"How are you feeling, baby," she asked.

"I'm confused, Mom," I replied. All I remember is feeling nauseous at school, Chanel walking me to the nurse's office and now I'm here.

Mom looked at me and said, "Sweetie, you're fine, you... you and the baby." I burst out in tears.

"What do you mean *baby*? I'm pregnant? No, this can't be," I cried, as Norris walked in.

"Hey…How you feelin'," he asked, hesitantly. By the way he acted, I could tell he knew the news already.

"Fine, but I would be better if you weren't here," I replied.

He put his head down and walked out the room, as Chanel and her mom ran behind him. So many thoughts were running through my head all at once.

Mom got up and said, "Now, honey, I understand you are upset; and honestly, I am too, but now is not the time to show it. We are all here to support the both of you. Yes, you are still young, yes, you are still in school and have a lot planned for your future but look at the bright side. Creation of life is a beautiful thing and being able to do so is such a blessing. You both have an amazing support system and we all will get through this together. With prayer, faith and patience, anything is possible."

Mom always said the most comforting words at the right time. Although I was a little relieved, tears constantly rolled down my cheeks. Michelle got up and gave me a hug and told me she loved me and that it would be alright. She always tried to act like an angel around Mom, and I knew it was fake as hell, but I took it.

A few moments later, the doctor walked in followed by Norris, Chanel and their mom, Ms. Sherlene.

"Good afternoon, Miss Anderson, my name is Dr. Saki. It's good to see you up and alert. How are you feeling?"

"I'm doing ok, I guess," I replied.

"I'm sure your family has told you already, but you're pregnant. That explains the nauseous feeling you had. You were also dehydrated, which caused you to faint. We did some blood work, along with an ultrasound and MRI, when you first came in. The blood work showed dehydration, but other than that, everything was normal. Being that you fell, I ordered the MRI of your brain to be sure you didn't cause injury and the MRI was normal as well. You are about 12 weeks pregnant, which puts you around three months along. The ultrasound showed a healthy baby, thus far. Nothing at all on the ultrasound concerned me."

"Praise the Lord, my God is good," Mom yelled out, in the background.

Dr. Saki continued, "Well, you are good to go home. The most important thing for you is to stay hydrated, eat and rest for the next couple of days. The nurse will come in and discharge you. She will have information on what I went over with you, along with my contact information in case you have any questions or concerns."

"Thank you," I replied.

After leaving, I went home and cried my eyes out. Pregnant?! I couldn't fuckin' believe it! I never thought I would be a teenage mom! I was one of those kids who did everything I was supposed to. I was scared to fuck up or do anything wrong. I couldn't believe I was pregnant, and then I looked down at my stomach and realized it was real!

I was still in high school, he was hours away in college, but that wasn't the only issue. I was just getting over this lying, cheating, no-good nigga. I would have to deal with him for almost the rest of my life. I wasn't wit' it! I never once thought an abortion would be an option for me, but neither was keeping Norris's baby, so it was the only choice I had.

That night, I went in Michelle's room and spoke to her about it. She was my big sister, and although we hated each other, I needed her. Luckily, she was on my side. She hated Norris anyway, so having a baby with him was like telling her I robbed a bank... The worse thing ever. She had a friend who went through with an abortion and she explained to me everything about it. The good and the bad. Surprisingly, Michelle even offered to take me. She hardly ever wanted to do anything for me, which was a bit strange, but I didn't put too much thought into it.

The next day, I told Mom that I decided to go with the abortion. She was enraged! She started preaching. Preaching about how abortions are a way of betraying God and how wrongful it was. It didn't change my mind, though. There was no way I was bringing a kid into the world I wasn't ready for. I refused to turn out to be an unfit parent, when I knew I wasn't ready from the beginning. Mom did not talk to me for two weeks. During that two weeks, I made my appointment and my procedure was being done the next week.

The week went by so fast. On the day of my procedure, Norris picked me up. I decided to put my feelings aside to get through it. I was grateful he was actually there for me and supporting me, although he wanted to keep the baby. It was hard for him. He was really excited to be a dad.

As we approached the office building, there were Christian protesters outside. There were some that walked up on the car, as we drove in the parking lot. There were some who stood along the streets. There were some that stood in front of the car even, so we could not drive in.

They all held up signs that read different things like "Don't do it!" "Don't kill your baby!"

They all were yelling things at me. One lady yelled, "God will never forgive you for this," as another yelled, "There is help, sweetie, there is other options. Why kill an innocent kid? Please, don't walk in there. It's not too late!" It was very overwhelming and frustrating! It was very uncomfortable to hear the things they said to people.

I just didn't get it. How could these "Christians" be out here judging others for a decision they were making, when they didn't know one's situation and what brought them there? That's not even the half, though. Walking into the building was terrifying as well, but during the procedure was worse.

When they called me back for the procedure, no one could come in the room with me. Not one person I actually knew to comfort me. I was in a big-ass, cold room with huge machines. I felt like I was about to be one of those frogs we dissected in science class back in the 7th grade.

They had me undress from the waist down with a drape over me, a nurse by my side, holding my hand and a strange doctor I've never met before between my legs.

The meds that they gave me was supposed to make me dizzy, calmer, less alert, and help with pain. Instead, I was only dizzy. I felt and heard everything that went on. I felt like a piece of meat on the table. I felt everything! I cried heavily! I screamed loudly! As loud as I could, actually; then, the nurse said it was almost over, and to keep it down!

How supportive, right?! It was the worst feeling I've ever felt. It was an experience I never wanted to experience again. I couldn't believe I was a teen mom in an abortion clinic. Never did I ever think I would be there.

As I sat in recovery, all I could think about was everything I went through with Norris. It seemed like all the pain I dealt with was because of him. I fucked around and gave this nigga my pussy at a young age, just for him to hurt me. I finally got over this jackass and now I was sitting in an abortion clinic because he fucked up and wasn't worth shit. I was glad it was all over, so I could finally leave that fuckboy alone.

By the time we left, the protestors were gone. Norris asked me how it went and how I felt. I immediately broke down in tears, as I explained everything that happened.

"I'm so sorry you had to go through that, baby. I'm sorry I wasn't able to be there and support you like I wanted to," Norris cried.

He grabbed my head, buried my face in his arms and placed his head on top of mine, as we cried together.

"This is the worst thing I have ever done, Norris. I will never forgive myself for this! God will never forgive me for this, like the protestors said," I cried.

"No, baby, no... don't say that," Norris replied, as he lifted his head off mine, looked in my face, wiping my tears.

"As long as you ask for forgiveness, you will be forgiven. We will get through this together! I love you," he continued.

As we started to pull off and head home, I saw flashbacks in my head from what happened. Norris checked on me the entire time. He took me to his place, so I could really relax. Chanel came to check on me, periodically, trying to make me laugh and cheer me up.

I could not eat, I could not sleep, I did not want to go to school or anything. I had never experienced depression, but at that moment, I knew it was real. I could not stop crying. The entire day played back in my head, over and over.

After months of recovery and many counseling sessions, I got myself back on track. I was focusing back on school again. I even started taking college classes for credits. I had mentally prepared myself to move forward from Norris and all our previous situations.

Mom and Dad finally forgave me for getting pregnant and getting the abortion. Norris had left to go back to college. He was playing sports again, and after the abortion and counseling, I cut all ties with him.

Chapter 4

"Blinded by Love"

S hortly after all the chaos, I applied for a job at Burger King part-time. I got the job and cherished every moment of working there. But of course, Michelle was hatin' and shit. She was too good to come pick me up from work. When she did, she bitched about being embarrassed by me and my "little job," as she called it. She would always say how it made us look broke. I didn't care what she thought about my job, as long as I was working and trying to make a way for myself, unlike her.

Chanel wanted a job too. Since I had the job, I plugged her in. I couldn't eat and watch my best friend starve - that wasn't me. She really needed the money. She helped her mom out with bills, and sometimes I would even give her half of my spending money to help them. I hated how good I had it sometimes. It made me mad how much my bitchy-ass sister took advantage of the life we lived because I watched my best friend and her family struggle so hard.

All summer, we worked. We saved up money and I bought my first car. It wasn't the best, nothing like the Mercedes Michelle drove, but I still valued it just as much. My senior year I was driving. I was beyond excited! Nobody could tell me shit. My little hooptie was everything to me.

Chanel and I spent a lot of time together. We worked together, went to school together and chilled at home together. When you saw me, you saw her, and vice versa. Man, that was my bitch! We were now seniors, so it was all work no play. We kept our heads in the books and we got money. We still tried to squeeze fun in, when we could, though.

We would have our girl time and sleepovers, just to laugh, gossip and talk about drama. If Chanel didn't have the tea, I did. Anything that went on, we knew about. We didn't have it as often as we used to, but when we did, we enjoyed ourselves. It normally ended up being on a Friday or Saturday night, after we got off work.

One Friday night, we got off early, so we went back to Chanel's house. Surprisingly, her mom was home; we weren't expecting her to be there. She almost never had a night off. That's not the weird part about it, though. She had her hair pinned up, her makeup was done nicely, she had on a nice, bodycon dress that came to the knees and hugged her curves with a thigh-high split. She looked really nice!

I'd never seen Ms. Sherlene dressed up like that in all the years I knew Norris and Chanel. We complimented her and asked her what she had planned. She told us she was asked on a date. Chanel and I looked at each other like, *who the hell was taking her out without our permission*. Right after she told us that, there was a knock at the door.

Chanel and I stood behind Ms. Sherlene, as she opened the door, eager to see who the guy was and what he looked like. She welcomed him in and introduced him to us. He was a really nice guy; well, he seemed to be. His name was Harold, he was five years younger than her, which made him 42, and he worked at the hotel with her as a maintenance man. They had been dating for four months, but with her busy schedule, she was never available to go on an actual date.

We were happy to see her home, but we were ready for her to leave. We always sneaked her wine when she wasn't home. Somehow, she never seemed to notice. Hanging with Chanel, I was a good girl gone bad. I had never drunk alcohol until I started hanging with her.

We laughed and talked, and I found out that her dude fucked up too, so she was just as single as I was. Chanel never gave second chances. Guys flocked to her. She was a pretty, redbone with a big ass. She could always get another, and she knew that, so she never gave a damn about cutting dudes off. From one guy to the next she went. Dropping them like flies and replacing them quicker than you could say her name.

She asked me what was up with Norris and me. She knew I wasn't fuckin' with him anymore, but she knew the kind of love I had for him too. She thought I went back on my word and gave in to his bullshit, once more, but I set it straight, without hesitating.

I could tell by the look she gave me that she didn't believe me. Damn! It was fucked up; sis really thought I was a weak link. But, after talking more about it, she realized I meant what I said and did exactly as I said I would. Cutting ties with Norris was the most difficult thing I could have done, but from that moment on, I started to learn my strength.

We started talking about how we needed to focus on finishing school and working. Keeping our head in the books and making money was our way of staying out of trouble. Chanel struggled in school. I helped her as much as I could, but many times, she talked about dropping out. I tried motivating her, keeping her straight and I even promised her that if she didn't attend college and all my dreams come true, I would be there for her… Hold her down, have her back, like a real friend was supposed to. The bond we had was one that I'd never imagined we would have, but it was unbreakable, and I could never see it any other way.

About three weeks later, Ms. Sherlene moved Mr. Harold in. Once he moved in, Chanel realized that he wasn't any good for her. She liked Mr. Harold, at first, but getting to really know him once he moved in showed her who he really was. After he got comfortable, he started falling off, taking advantage of Chanel's mom and he became baggage. Everyone could see he wasn't worth shit, except the person he mattered to the most.

It started to tear Chanel and her mom apart because she would always take up for him and somehow blame things on Chanel. Her mom believed everything he said. She knew her kids disliked him, so she never wanted to hear anything they had to say about him.

I knew she wanted happiness, and she deserved it too, but it was fucked up she ignored her kids' feelings about the guy. Her mom would always tell her, "You're just exaggerating, you're trying to find every reason not to like him. You're just an outsider looking in. He is not that bad."

When Harold moved in, it put a damper on their relationship, and her own mom was blind to it. We didn't know what Harold had done or said to Chanel's mom, but he had her where he wanted her. She did everything he asked, she believed everything he said, and she was even abandoning her own kids for him. She was doing everything she said she would never do if she got a man. It was sad. She was becoming a person we didn't know.

Chanel was so upset and uncomfortable in her own home, she pretty much moved in with my family. My parents were fine with it and welcomed her in with open arms. We had a guest bedroom where she could have her own space and privacy, but she insisted on staying in my room. I had two beds in there, so it all worked out perfectly. She still went home from time to time to get things she needed.

As time went on, Harold got worse and Chanel hated him more. He would either be mean to her for no reason or say slick shit. One day, she went home to grab some clothes, and when we walked in, he said, "Well, hi to y'all too, little disrespectful bitches."

We didn't say anything to him, we didn't even look at him, we just kept walking. Chanel and I went in her room, so she could get the clothes that she went there for. I always went with her because neither of us trusted him. I would not allow her to ever go there alone. As we walked out, Harold asked Chanel, "What you got in that bag?"

"None of your business, asshole," Chanel mumbled under her breath. We both laughed, as we walked out of the house.

"What the hell is his problem," I asked Chanel.

"He's a fuckin' weirdo. I don't even know why my mama likes him! I just don't get it. It's like, I don't even know her anymore. After Harold, she turned into a monster. Now, she is just as much of an asshole as he is, I swear," Chanel cried.

"How could she allow a stranger to come in our home and tear our family apart? How," Chanel continued.

I pulled the car over. Chanel placed her head on my shoulder. Grabbing her hand with one of my hands and wiping her tears with the other, I tried calming her.

"Chanel, look at me! It's going to be ok, I promise," I said to her.

I thought about a place I went to be free, so I decided to take Chanel there. It was a nice, relaxing place where she could calm down. It was a place where I always went alone at night. I started going there as a young kid. I found it just wandering off and had been going ever since. I don't think anybody knew about it, which made it so special.

I went when I had a lot on my mind and when I wanted a peaceful, relaxing environment. This place helped me get through life itself. When we arrived at our destination, Chanel looked at me with a strange, puzzled look on her face. I laughed hard because she didn't understand.

"Really, Tara, the park," Chanel said.

I just giggled, got out the car and grabbed her by the arm, yelling, "Yes, really, the park... now, let's go!"

It looked like an ordinary park with a huge field, a gated play area with swings, slides, monkey bars, seesaws, and etc. but this was no ordinary park to me. It was a place near the back of the park where a few trees were.

The place was nice now. There were beautiful flowers. I planted one folding chair because I often came alone, and I would bring a blanket to lay on, when I wanted to gaze at the stars, listen to chirping birds and enjoy the cool breeze.

I was able to overcome all the tough issues that I went through that I never saw myself healing from. This place was therapeutic for me. It was very special. It really was, so with Chanel having so much on her plate at once, I felt that sharing my secret getaway with her would be beneficial. It was free and close to her home, so she could even walk here if she'd like.

As we walked to the secret getaway, I told her how it helped me and how nobody knew about the place except for myself and now her. I told her how important it was that it remained that way. She promised me she would never share it. As we approached the trees, Chanel started getting nervous.

"It's ok, I promise," I whispered to Chanel.

"Ok," Chanel replied, hesitantly.

We started to reach the end of the path and Chanel just stared at me. "Welcome to paradise," I told her, as I giggled!

"This is my getaway, Tara? You can't be serious right now," Chanel said.

As I looked at her and grinned, I said, "You can't look at it as a park, Chanel. It's so much more than that. Soon, you will understand!"

We stayed for just a little bit, lying on the ground with blankets underneath us, listening to the birds chirp. We cried, we talked, and we laughed. Although I knew she would not admit that this place was pretty nice and wasn't so bad, I could tell she enjoyed it. We left and went back to my crib.

As I was driving, Chanel asked, "What made you share your getaway with me?"

"Because, you are my girl, I trust you and you needed this. Unfortunately, we can't afford a really nice getaway right now, but this was the closest thing to it. I saw you needed it and I just wanted to help. That's what friends are for," I replied.

She leaned over, kissed me on the cheek and said, "You know, Tara, I'm really happy we squashed our beef and became really close. You are like the sister I always wanted. Your family has the perfect life I always wanted, and I just don't know where I would be without any of you right now! Who would have ever known we would be so close? We hated each other!" We both started laughing.

"I know, Chanel, it's so crazy, but you know...."

"Everything happens for a reason," Chanel chimed in.

"I knew you would say that, you always say that. And like you always say too, "One day, I will understand," she continued.

"Absolutely," I replied, as we walked in the door to my house.

As we got through our senior year, days, weeks, even months went by and things were getting better for us. Chanel was getting better, mentally. She still wasn't speaking to her mom; in fact, it was almost two months since she even went by the house. She spoke to Norris frequently, though.

He was still busy at school. He didn't like Harold either, so he hardly ever came home. I was over Norris completely. We actually started talking as friends, with less tension, and we were more cordial with one another.

Time flew by and we were graduating high school. As a graduation gift, my parents bought me a new car, gave Chanel my old car and offered to pay her tuition for college, as long as she kept her grades up. We had found a college two hours away from home, and actually 30 mins away from the college Norris attended.

We both planned to do two years there. I was going to take up nursing and Chanel was going for early childhood. We both had already gotten accepted, so we just had to get through the summer, and we would be off to a new journey and new beginnings. We had planned to keep our jobs and work in the summer and on school breaks. Our manager was fine with that. She was willing to work with us, knowing we were college students now.

Two weeks into summer, I was working almost every day. Chanel wasn't, now that she didn't have to. She wanted to enjoy summer break. Everything was going well… until one day I was at work. Chanel texted me and asked if I wanted to go to the movies and I told her yes.

She said, "Let's meet at the mall around 5pm to get some outfits."

It worked out really well because I got off at 2. I could take a nap and then go to the mall. I did just that.

I got there around 4:30pm and I texted Chanel to let her know I was a little early, but I was there. After 10 minutes, she didn't respond back and that wasn't like her. I still sat in the parking lot in the car in front of the mall. Five more minutes went pass and she still didn't text me back. I called her, she didn't answer. I started to get worried because that wasn't like her to not answer the phone or even text back. She told me that morning she had errands to run, but she didn't get into details about it.

Chapter 5

"Sick Bastard"

I called Mom and asked her if she knew what time Chanel left the house. She said around 10am and told me she hadn't seen her since. I said ok. Mom asked me what was wrong, but I told her nothing. I didn't want to worry her, if it really was nothing. She said, "Ok," again, and then hung up. I called Chanel three more times. She still didn't answer. At that point, it was 5:40pm and I was still sitting in the parking lot. I called Norris and asked him if he spoke to her. He said he did earlier. I left the mall and went to Chanel's mom's house.

Her mom was just getting home. She said, "Hey, sweetie. Where's Chanel?"

I told her I wasn't sure and that was the reason I came over.

"We had plans to meet at the mall, but she didn't show. I was coming by to see if she was here."

"Well, I'm just getting home from work, let me ask Harold if she came by," Ms. Sherlene replied.

She walked in the house, as I followed her in.

"Harold?! Harold," Chanel's mom yelled.

"Have you seen Chanel at all today? Did she come by the house while I was at work?"

"No, baby, I…I haven't seen Chanel all…all day today," Mr. Harold stuttered.

As I was heading out, I started to get on my phone and call around, but I was interrupted by Chanel's mom.

"Hey, Tara, wait! I'm worried about Chanel! Do you think she is ok? Should I call the cops? Can you call me if-" Chanel's mom was so startled I had to interrupt her.

"Calm down, Ms. Sherlene. I know you're worried. I am too, but I'm sure she's fine. Hold off on calling the police. Let me run to the house, do some thinking about where she could possibly be and make some calls. I will call you, if anything changes; and when she shows up at the house, I'll be sure to have her call you as well," I said.

"Thank you, Tara, thank you so much for all your help! Please, call me, sweetie, and drive safe," Chanel's mom cried.

"I will. Thank you, Ms. Sherlene. Talk to you soon."

I got in the car and started thinking. My mind started racing. I sat in the car and the conversation Chanel's mom and Mr. Harold had played back in my head. I had so many questions. Why didn't he seem concerned about where she was? Why was he stuttering? Why did he seem so nervous and got sweaty all of a sudden? He just didn't seem normal and it wasn't sitting right with me.

As thoughts continued to run threw my head, my phone rang. It was Norris. He called to check on Chanel and to see if I had gotten in contact with her already. I told him I didn't and that I was just leaving their mom's house. He told me he was going to head down to help look for her and for me to call him if I found her.

"I will. See you when you get here and drive safe," I replied.

I drove through the neighborhood, went to some of Chanel ex boyfriends' houses and drove through their neighborhoods, but there was still no sign of Chanel. I went to the house and Mom was there.

"Did you talk to Chanel, Tara? What's going on," Mom asked.

"I haven't, Mom. We were supposed to meet at the mall around five and go out tonight, but she never showed at the mall. She didn't answer any of my calls and she never responded to my text and that's not like her. "

"I called Norris and he hasn't spoken to her since earlier. I went by her ex-boyfriend's house and she wasn't there either. I did go to her mom's house, but she wasn't there."

"Ms. Sherlene was just getting home, and she asked Mr. Harold if Chanel came by, but he said he hadn't seen her. He told us that, but something just doesn't seem right, Ma. Ms. Sherlene was extremely worried, and we talked outside for a while, but he showed no sympathy or concern about her disappearance. She may believe everything he tells her, but I don't! I am trying to stay optimistic, like you, Mom, and be strong for everybody and not think the worst, but I'm getting worried, Mom! I just hope she's ok! I hope we find her soon! I need to find her! I need answers," I cried.

"I know, baby. Chanel is ok, I can feel it, and we will find her soon," Mom replied, as she hugged me.

Michelle walked in. "What's going on? What's wrong with Tara, Mom," she asked.

"Apparently, Chanel is nowhere to be found and she's just worked up and worried," Mom told her.

Chanel's mom called multiple times. Norris already came down and he was over there with her, comforting her. As I sat in the house, something came to me. I jumped up, grabbed my keys and left out the door.

"Where are you going, Tara," Michelle yelled.

"To find my friend," I hollered back.

When I pulled up to the park, I didn't see Chanel's car. I sat there, and tears started rolling down my cheeks, as I banged my head against the steering wheel. I was clueless to where she could be at that point. I was almost confident that I could find her there. I started to back my car up to leave, then I pulled back in the parking spot. I got out the car and went in the back to the hideaway. There, Chanel was balled up, sitting on the ground, crying.

"Chanel? Friend? Is that you? I can't believe you are here! You have everyone worried! What are you doing here," I cried.

"Tara…I just want to be alone," Chanel wept.

"Chanel, what's wrong," I asked.

"Tara…Just…Just leave me alone," Chanel yelled, as she started to get up.

"Chanel, I understand you are upset, but I'm here for you! Out of all people, I should be the person you open up to! I've never seen you like this! I've been worried about you all day and I just wanna know what's wrong," I said to her, firmly.

Chanel stood there, listening to me, as she cried. Then, moments later, she took off running. I didn't know where she was headed, but I went behind her. She kept running and I stayed on her. She got to the street, went across, and then dropped in the grass.

She looked me in my eyes, as she started to cry, hysterically, and said, "Tara, he raped me! He raped me!"

"Oh my! Chanel, who did this to you? Who the fuck did it? Tell me now!" I said, furiously.

Chanel hesitated, as she sat, balled up on the ground with her face buried in her knees.

"It was Mr. Harold, wasn't it? I knew it! Something didn't sit right with me. His story sounded like bullshit and his words and actions wasn't adding up."

"What…What are you talking about, Tara," Chanel cried.

"I'll explain later. Now, let's go…Now, Chanel," I yelled.

As I was thinking about what the next move was, I grabbed Chanel's arm and pulled her along with me. When we got in the car, my phone rang. It was Norris. He was over at my mom's house.

"Hey, Tara. Where you at? Did you find Chanel," Norris asked.

"Are my babies ok," Mom yelled, in the background.

"Tell Mom we're fine and I have Chanel. We are on the way and shit is real! We have no time, tell everybody throw on their shoes. When I get there, make sure everyone is ready," I said, furiously!

"Ready for what, Tara? You need to chill. What's going on," Norris asked.

"I'll tell you when I get there. Just make sure everyone is ready, we pullin' up in seven," I said, before hanging up the phone.

I was speeding to get to the house. My adrenaline was pumping, and I was ready to kick Mr. Harold's ass myself!

"Tara, please calm down. You're scaring me. I've never seen you like this," Chanel cried.

"Chanel, you don't understand. When I went by your mom's house to see if you were there, your mom was just getting home when I pulled up and she asked Mr. Harold if he had seen you today. He looked me in my eyes and fuckin' lied! I'm tired of being lied to! He didn't show concern like Ms. Sherlene did. He didn't offer to help find you. I knew something wasn't right. He is a weird-ass dude and we've been sick of him for a long time now. He hit below the belt with this one and I'm not going to ease up at all."

"This is bullshit! Fuckin' bullshit, Chanel! Your mom's boyfriend raped you! No, girl, woman, anyone deserves to go through that shit," I hollered.

"But you can't tell my mom. She won't believe me! I'm begging you, Tara," Chanel cried.

"Well, he is getting his ass beat tonight, so she will find out. You also need to go to the hospital and he needs to be locked up tonight! I respect how you feel, Chanel, but one way or another, she will find out."

We pulled up to the house and I pulled Chanel along with me. She didn't want to go in the house. She was embarrassed.

"I got you, Chanel. We have to let them know what happened," I told her.

Mom heard the car door slam shut, so she ran to the door and opened it for us. Everybody came out and started hugging us.

"Let's go inside, y'all," I told them all.

Mom hugged Chanel and held her and so did Michelle. Norris was so happy to see her; he cried and kissed her forehead like a million times.

"Do you want me to tell them or you prefer to do so," I asked Chanel.

"What happened, sweetie," Mom asked, looking back and forth at Chanel and I.

"Who did this to you, Nelly?" Norris asked.

"I had to get away," Chanel said, as tears started rolling down her face, again.

"Why, Chanel," Norris asked.

"Did someone hurt you," Norris asked, again, hardly giving her time to speak.

"Calm down, Norris, let her speak," Michelle yelled!

"I was raped by...by Mr. Harold! Tara and I had plans to go to the movies and have a good night tonight, since she got off early. I went by the house to get some shoes I wanted to wear tonight. I didn't know he was there because he wasn't in the living room like he normally is. I went in the room and grabbed my shoes fast, before he came home or something. As I was walking out the room, he was walking out the bathroom. He started saying weird things to me...as he normally does. I didn't say anything back, I just walked off. Then, he grabbed my arm. He said, 'So you just gon' walk off like you don't hear me talking to you? I said, you look pretty today, you can at least say thank you.' He pushed me against my room door. I yelled, let me go, several times, as I tried to get away from him, but he held me tight."

"Then, he said, 'I will, once you give me what I've always wanted'." He started unbuckling his belt and pulled out his private. He started pulling my pants and underwear down, as he whispered in my ear, 'You always mess with these little boys around here, but me, I'm a grown-ass man. Your momma told me you always asked her why she's even with me. You asked that, huh?' I was in disbelief of what was going on and all I could yell was let me go! I tried fighting him off the entire time, but it wasn't working. He pushed his private in me and said, 'Maybe this is why yo' momma with me'," Chanel cried, rapidly.

"Oh my!" Mom cried.

I was speechless. I held my mouth and stood with my back against the wall, in disgust. I couldn't believe this. I never doubted he would do something like that to someone because he was weird like that. It was just agonizing to sit there and hear what my friend had experienced. It was too much. I couldn't take it.

Norris stormed out the house.

"Norris, wait! Where are you going," Mom yelled.

"He's gone, y'all," Michelle said to us, seconds later.

"Please, somebody go get him! Norris has a bad temper," Chanel yelled.

I jumped in my car and followed him. Mom, Chanel and Michelle came right behind us in Michelle's car. Mom called the police, while in the car. The plan was for us to tell Ma what happened, so she could call the cops and Chanel could go to the hospital; but after hearing what happened, there was a slight delay in the process.

Norris lead us to his mom's house. He jumped out the car, while it was still on, and repeatedly pounded on Ms. Sherlene's door. She answered the door, but when she opened it, she asked, "Norris, what is wrong?"

He didn't speak, instead, he pushed her to the side and walked around the house yelling, "Where is that bitch?"

"Now, you are going to respect my home or leave, Norris. Watch your damn mouth in here," Ms. Sherlene hollered back.

When he walked in the back to his mom's room, he found Mr. Harold lying down, watching TV. He always had the TV loud, so he didn't hear anything that was going on. Chanel's mom ran behind him.

Norris went in the room and punched Mr. Harold in his face. As they fought, Chanel's mom was in the back, yelling, "Stop, Norris! Y'all stop this bullshit!"

I went in the house and went in the back where they were.

When Michelle, Mom and Chanel pulled up, the door was wide open. Mom came running in and behind her was Michelle. It was chaotic. When Mom came in, Norris and I was whipping Mr. Harold's ass. Ms. Sherlene grabbed me by my shirt, as I was kicking him.

"Get your hands off my damn child," Mom yelled at Ms. Sherlene.

Michelle tried grabbing Norris. Mom and Ms. Sherlene started arguing, and while Michelle grabbed Mom, I went in the car with Chanel to comfort her.

She was in tears. So much had happened. As the cops pulled up, we heard gunshots. I tried to get out the car, but a cop stopped me. The three other cops went inside.

Chanel yelled, "Who got shot?"

She started pounding on the car window and kept saying, "Who got shot? Who got shot?"

"Ma'am, please, calm down. I can't let you out the vehicle right now," the officer told Chanel.

Although I was just as worried as she was, I tried to calm her down. We started hearing sirens, and then an ambulance and fire truck showed up. Mom and Michelle walked out, talking to one officer that went in the house. Chanel's mom walked out with the other officer. They rolled out a stretcher and Norris was on it. The last officer had Mr. Harold in cuffs, as they walked him out.

The cop that stood outside the car door finally opened it and let us out. I ran to Mom and Chanel started screaming for Norris, as she ran towards him. Cops started grabbing her, demanding her to back off and calm down. They closed the ambulance door and rushed Norris to the hospital.

Ms. Sherlene ran up to Chanel, trying to comfort and calm her, but she refused to speak to her. In fact, she started flipping out more. Mom walked up to them and told Ms. Sherlene to leave Chanel alone for the moment. Surprisingly, Ms. Sherlene listened, without putting up a fight.

The cop that Michelle and Mom was talking to started asking us questions. They needed a statement from everybody, before we could leave. Once we gave our statements, they took Mr. Harold away. They checked Chanel out in another ambulance and wanted to transport her to the hospital for further evaluation. She denied her mom's request to ride in the ambulance with her and asked that Mom and I go instead. Ms. Sherlene followed behind us in her own car.

Chapter 6

"Crazy Shit"

We all were in the hospital room more concerned about Norris, after finding out Chanel was ok. We didn't know where he was shot, if he was going to live, or what to expect, if and when, we were able to see him.

"Chanel? How are you feelin'," I asked.

"I'm Ok, I guess."

"Will you talk to your mom when she gets here," Michelle asked.

"I don't want to. I know she wasn't there when it happened, but it's still her fault what happened to Norris and I! I know she won't believe me. She never wants to hear what we have to say about him! I'm fuckin' pissed with her! I'm just annoyed that she really doesn't care about us, when at one point... well, all my life, we were all she had! I thought a mother's love was unconditional, but I haven't felt it in months," Chanel sobbed.

"You won't have to worry about him anymore," Michelle replied.

"I love y'all," Chanel whispered.

We all sat there, hugging for a while, and then there was a knock on the room door.

The door opened, slowly, and Chanel picked her head up lightly, as Michelle and I turned to look.

"Hey, baby," Ms. Sherlene whispered.

Chanel sat there, silently, with a grimaced look on her face, as she rolled her eyes.

"Can y'all give us a minute," Ms. Sherlene asked.

Before we could respond, Chanel did.

"Hell no! You are lucky I'm giving you a minute; now, say what you have to say, while my family is in here, or don't speak at all!"

I could see the vexed look on Ms. Sherlene's face, as her eyes grew wide.

"I'm so sorry this happened to you, baby. I never thought this would happen. I feel like I failed as a parent. Not being able to protect you…" Ms. Sherlene wept.

"You did! It wouldn't have happened, if your selfish-ass had listened to us about him from the beginning," Chanel shouted.

Michelle and I just sat there. We didn't know what to say or do. Moments later, the room door opened; that time, it was Mom.

"Mom!" I whispered, breathing in relief.

"We need you; it's like a Jerry Springer show in this room, I announced, as I pointed. Please, I'm begging you," I said quietly, but sternly.

Mom opened the door and yelled, "Hey," but Chanel and Ms. Sherlene were still going at it. They didn't hear Mom's diminutive voice speaking.

"You ruined my damn life! I was finally happy! You and Norris just had to come in between us and run my man off," Ms. Sherlene yelled.

Our mouths dropped, in shock!

"It's your damn fault! You are a sorry, piece of shit, just like him! Go on, run off and be with him. I know you will! Ol' desperate bitch," Chanel hollered back. Then, her mom smacked her.

Mom jumped in between them.

"Now, I don't condone violence, but if any one of you hit me, oh, it's on and poppin'," Mom said.

I giggled, softly, and Michelle looked at me and asked, "Well, where did she learn that," as we both laughed.

Mom went on.

"Enough is enough! You are a child, Chanel. I understand you are upset, but you need to respect your mother. For you, Sherlene, you need to also show her respect and accept how she feels. She is going through a lot and this little girl is damaged! She's damaged for God's sake!"

"Understand that it is not something that is easy to process and deal with. On the other hand, you have another child in here that is in the ICU fighting for his life. How about you put the bullshit aside for now and take care of your responsibilities! There is a time and a place for everything, but now is not the time nor the place," Mom preached.

Mom wanted us to leave and get some rest. She was going to stay and make sure Norris was okay, but Chanel refused.

"I'm not leaving until I see my brother," Chanel screamed.

We calmed her down and stayed. It was going on 3 a.m. and we all were in the waiting area, waiting to hear from a nurse or doctor about Norris. None of us was able to see him since he'd gotten there. Not knowing what was going on with him in the back, we prayed.

"Father God, I ask that you watch over him, Lord. Heal him and protect him. Father, I ask that his surgery goes well, and he wakes up fine from anesthesia. I ask that the nurses and doctors focus on him and everything is done properly. In Jesus' name we pray. Amen."

Hours went by, but we still heard nothing. Nurses came from out back to get families, but none came for us. We began to worry. Chanel started to panic, and Ms. Sherlene cried. I never gave up hope. I was replaying in my head the moments Norris and I had. The good and the bad. I smiled, closed my eyes and said a prayer of my own.

The double doors opened, again. The nurse came from out back towards the waiting room with a medical chart in her hand. We all stared, hoping they would be calling us. She looked down at the chart, looked back up and yelled, "Smith Family."

We all jumped up! Our prayers were answered. It was our time. She took us back to his room. Not knowing what condition he was in, we got nervous. As we walked down the cold, silent hallway, I ran my hands across the hall rails. I was shaking and anxious to see him. I was trying to mentally prepare myself for what we were about to see.

When we walked in, Chanel started crying. I can't even front, my eyes started watering as well; I was thinking about how much I loved him and how close I was to losing a friend forever. It was hard seeing Norris in the hospital bed, hooked up to machines, lying lifeless in the bed.

Norris stayed in the hospital for a couple of weeks. After Norris found out that he couldn't play college football anymore

- which was what held the majority of his scholarships, he dropped out. Ms. Sherlene wasn't paying for it. Norris couldn't afford it, so dropping out was his only option.

He stayed with Steven, one of his best friends. Norris had no income, so he started stressin' about what his next move would be. Sports was all he knew. That was his only interest. The gunshot wound to his chest almost took his life, and from that day on, Norris' life was changed forever. After recovering, Norris linked back up with some dudes from the high school. He had a couple homeboys back in the hood he chilled with too.

Norris was one of the few niggas who made it out the hood and had a bright future ahead of him. He didn't have a record, never got in trouble with the police and didn't have beef in the streets; but after dropping out of college and hanging with his old click, he got caught up in their shit. He started drug dealing, gun toting, smoking and drinking. I didn't know who he was anymore.

Chanel was still stressing out about everything that happened. With the court date slowly approaching, she was petrified, not knowing what to expect, hoping justice would be served.

When the court date came, everybody went. When we arrived at court, Chanel's mom was there, but she sat on the opposite side from us, supporting Mr. Harold instead (Yeah, that was awkward as fuck. I never understood that, but whatever). The judge found him guilty of first degree rape and he was sentenced to 25 years. Chanel's mom ran out of the court room crying. Chanel was filled with tears of joy and relieved that justice was being served.

Time flew by! Two years went by quicker than I thought, and so much had changed. I went to college and graduated. I started out majoring in nursing but realized that wasn't where my heart was, although I dreamed of becoming a nurse since I could remember. I ended up changing my major to business management and graduated with that degree. I moved back with my parents and started working in the real estate office that mom worked at. It wasn't where I dreamed of working, but it was a start.

Michelle had already graduated from the school, but she was working at a dentist office as a receptionist, never using her degree. Her and her best friends, Allie and Gina, were living together, drinking and partying almost every night of the week.

Chanel never started college, but she was doing much better. She was going to therapy, which seemed to help. Her and Norris ended up moving in together. Chanel had a better job. She gave up McDonald's and was working at the Michael Kors store as a shift manager. I guess her bullying and bossiness all paid off. I was proud of her.

Norris was still on his same ol' bullshit. Hustling full-time, selling dope, weed and prescription pills. He'd change so much, being in the game. I never thought he would be a street nigga, but shit, he had to do what he had to do.

I was at Chanel's house a lot. I was in the process of moving out myself, but it was taking more time than I thought. I would go over to her place when I got off work. I spent nights there, and almost every day I was off I was there.

Norris and I were in a good place. He still flirted with me from time to time, but he knew he didn't stand a chance. Besides, he had already ruined all the ones he had. I was also not trying to live a drug life and potentially lose everything I had worked hard for, anyways.

Chanel and I was around Norris and his homeboys so much, I started to feel like a homeboy myself. We all chilled, played cards and drank together. We would even go out every so often with Norris, Steven, Josh and Rocko. We had so much fun with them. That was our circle. We didn't have many female friends, all we had was one another. The guys were who we hung with; and no matter what, they always made sure we were good.

One Saturday night, I was off. I was at their house and we all decided, last minute, to go out, since we were bored. We road in two, separate cars. Chanel and I were together, and the guys were in the other. We went to a spot Downtown that Norris went to a lot. It was ratchet as hell, but security was tight, there were deals on the drinks and the hookah were cheap. We stayed for a while. We all drank, we danced, and we had a good time.

When we left, we were walking back to the cars. Chanel and I were ahead of the rest of them. When we turned around to make sure they were good, we saw these two, drunk ladies walking up to them. They looked like junkies. They looked a mess and, sure enough, they asked the guys if they knew anyone who had some crack.

Norris sold crack, but he had his clients. He was very apprehensive and cautious about who he sold to, so they said no. The guys joked about it, as they drunk-asses stumbled more than the women. After trippin' off the women, they all walked off, except Josh. He was so drunk he stood there, laughing and talking to them. Steven had to go and get him.

When Steven went back, he looked at the ladies in their faces hard. He stood there for a while and whispered, "Hold up! Ms. Sherlene, that's you?" As he said that, her eyes got wide. He yelled for Norris to come over. Norris walked over and then Chanel and I followed him.

"Hey, bro, I think that's your mom," Steven said to Norris.

Norris looked in her face and said, "Momma? Momma! Look at me! So, you fuckin' with crack now? What the fuck," Norris yelled at her.

"Norris, hey, man, I've been trying to call you. I love you, son, and I miss you so much! How you been doing?"

Chanel and I just stood there.

"You don't give a fuck about me, you stopped calling before I was even healed! That was three years ago," Norris continued.

"I'm sorry, man. You know I love you! You got $20 I can borrow?"

"For what? For crack?"

"Well, just give me a little piece. I heard you got the best shit out here, man," his mom continued to beg.

"Hell no! Get your ass on! Get your supply from somewhere else. I'm not giving you drugs and I'm damn sure not giving you money for drugs! You need to get yourself together! I can't believe this shit," Norris yelled at her, as he walked off.

He was furious. To see how much she had let herself go and how hard she was on drugs tore him apart. She used to drink, when she could, but she never did drugs. He was really bothered.

Norris and Chanel were both embarrassed. He started yelling and cursing, as we walked back to our cars. Boxing on his car, Norris grew angrier. Everyone tried to calm him down, but it wasn't much anybody could do. We all were drunk as hell. He got in the car and just started crying.

"Let me talk to him! Just stand here," Chanel said to us. We all stood outside, as the two of them sat in the car and talked.

"I can't believe this shit! I thought that was her, but I had to look twice. He's out here dealing drugs to somebody else's family members and now somebody else is out here dealing drugs to his mom. Man, the shit is so crazy, man," Steven said, in disappointment.

"I know he's hurting! They both are. Chanel might not show it, but I've known her long enough to know. Although she doesn't speak to her mom or have a relationship with her, it still hurts her," I said.

Interrupted in our conversation, Chanel stuck her head out the door and told us she would take him home and that she would meet us at the house, leaving me stuck with Norris' drunk-ass friends.

Chapter 7

"Lingering Love"

I got a call that my condo was ready. Taking care of everything, immediately, I was able to move in the upcoming weekend. Since I was settled in, I planned a housewarming for the weekend after. It was my first time being on my own, so it was a must I celebrated.

All my family and friends came. Josh brought his two brothers, Chris and Chase, who I'd never met before. A few of my cousins even came. It was a nice turnout.

Mom and Dad left, and we all partied and got drunk afterwards.

"Hey, Tara, this is my oldest brother, Chris, and youngest brother, Chase. I hope you don't mind me bringing them along," Josh said.

"Nice to meet you," Chase and Chris said, at the same time.

"Likewise," I replied, to them both.

"No, no problem at all, Josh, it's cool," I told him.

Everyone brought gifts. I needed them. My place was damn near empty. Shit, I ain't have it like that! Free shit was always the best shit. Everything that was bought was a few bucks

I kept in my pockets and it was appreciated. Everybody was having a good time. Going out to clubs was cool and all, but it couldn't compare to a good, old-fashioned house party. Having so much fun and not giving a fuck about how drunk I already was, I went in the kitchen to get another beer, and then Chris walked up on me.

"Nice place," he said.

"Well, thank you. It took a long time for me to find this place, but it was worth the wait. Where do you live, if you don't mind me askin'?"

"Oh, I live in Atlanta, pursuing my career, but I'm from Charlotte. Just down visiting family."

"Oh, that's nice. I've never been to Atlanta. What kind of industry are you in?"

"The club and entertainment business."

"Oh, that's nice. If you ever need a business manager, I can definitely help with that," I said, blushing.

Chris laughed. "I'll keep that in mind. So, is that what you do?"

"Yeah, I graduated with an Associate's in business management. I'm going to eventually open my own business."

"Ok, boss lady! That's wassup, shawty. I like that! Chase yo' dream, it's worth it. So, if I'm interested in you managing my business, how can I get in contact with you?"

I snatched a piece of paper off my counter, wrote down my email address and handed it to him. Chris looked at me with a puzzled look on his face. He thought he was getting my number, with those whack-ass lines he came to me with, he could think again. I was drunk, but I wasn't dumb. I'd been there and done that. He was a smooth-talker, just like Norris was and I refused to go down that route again.

As I handed him my email address on a paper, Josh walked up.

"Well, well, what do we have here," Josh asked.

"Just networking," Chris told him.

"Yeah, just networking," I said to Josh as well.

"Did you know she majored in business management," Chris asked Josh.

"Yeah, I sure did! Looks like more than business to me, though, but I'm going to just mind my business and go back to the party," Josh replied, as he walked off, winking.

Josh left and then Norris came over, less than two minutes later.

"Hitting on my girl, huh, Chris," Norris asked.

"Oh no, man, we were just networking. My bad, bro, I didn't know y'all were dating," Chris said.

"We're not! He's just an annoying ex," I replied, quickly.

"She's still my girl, though. We have a connection, you know," Norris replied, and then kissed me on the cheek.

"Go sit yo' drunk-ass down, Norris," I said, as I wiped my cheek off with my shirt.

"Ok, baby, I'm going, I'm going!"

I rolled my eyes and continued on with the conversation Chris and I were having.

"Yeah, that was years ago. I'm sorry."

"You must be something special, if it's been that long and he's not over you yet!"

"Of course, I am," I said, as I walked off, leaving Chris in the kitchen, wondering.

I went back to the party and continued to enjoy myself. Next thing I know, one night of a housewarming turned into a damn sleepover. We all had a good time. Too much of a good time. They were too intoxicated to drive home, and I was so intoxicated I allowed them to stay, without knowing. It never fails, black people always overstay their welcome, but it turned out to be lots of fun, though. Besides, it was fine. In my eyes, everyone there was family and welcomed anytime.

When I woke up, I didn't realize it was Sunday. Mom wanted to kill me! I was missing church for the third time in a row. Michelle jumped up when Allie and Gina woke her and ran straight out the door, leaving it up to me to drop them off home.

"When is the next house party, Tara," Gina asked.

"Girl, I'm just so busy with everything, I hardly have time for myself… let alone a party," I replied.

"Your place is really cute and comfy. I hope you enjoy the gift," Allie said.

"I'm sure I will. I appreciate it. Thanks, again, for coming," I told them.

They left out the car and I went home to gather myself. I was so hungover. I couldn't believe how much alcohol I had consumed the night before. I hadn't drunk like that in a long time. Since the college parties, actually.

Chanel called me on the way home.

"Hello," I answered.

"Hey, girl, what you doin'? I wanted to come back by later!"

"Girl, I will have to let you know, I'm so hungover and tired. I just want to relax, since I work tomorrow. I just dropped Gina and Allie off at home because Michelle was so messed up she ran out the house this morning, forgetting she brought two, other human beings with her."

"What's wrong with her?"

"Oh, nothing, she was almost late for church and you know how Mom go about that. I haven't been to church the past three Sundays, so I'm sure I'm going to get a phone call in a few hours."

"Oh yeah, most definitely," Chanel replied, as we both laughed.

"I saw how you and Chris was chatting up a storm last night, what was that about," Chanel asked.

(I knew she wasn't calling me to just check up on me. She normally texted for something like that. I knew my friend well).

"Girl, we were just networking. He told me he lives in Atlanta, pursuing his career, so I asked what he does. He told me, then I told him my professional background. That condo, nor my future business will pay for itself, so I need all the money I can get."

"I know that's right!"

"He is kind of cute, and a really sweet guy, but he was also too smooth and seems manipulative. I'm just approaching with caution," I told her.

"He really is sweet though, Tara, and fine as hell… let me just throw that in there! Josh never said anything bad about him, and the few times I've been around him, he was always laughing or quiet. He is really chill and laid-back. Really cool guy. I think you should date him."

I was just looking to work with him, damn, but here she was, trying to convince me to date a nigga I just met.

"But that's Norris' friend, Chanel. How would that look on me?"

"No, Tara, let's be clear. That is Norris' best friend's brother. Not Norris' friend… I'm just sayin'," Chanel argued.

"Yeah, you are right in a way...Hold up, no, I'm not dating him, so it doesn't matter. He actually tried to get my number last night and I didn't give it to him...I gave him my email instead," I said, hesitantly.

"Your email? What the fuck, Tara? Who the hell gives a fine-ass dude with lots of money an email? Who taught you that," Chanel hollered.

"I knew I shouldn't have told you that. Now, I'm embarrassed!"

"I'm not judging. I love you and all, but that was a stupid-ass move. If his fine-ass had asked for my number, I probably would have gave up some ass too," Chanel joked.

As weeks went by, I started thinking about how long it'd been since I dated. I did get a good vibe from Chris and he was really cute. However, if I had the opportunity to work with him, I would rather do so, and I didn't want to mix business with pleasure. He hadn't emailed me yet either. Maybe I did ruin it by not giving him a number, or he truly wasn't into me.

I still couldn't get it out my head that he was my ex-boyfriend's best friend's brother. Taking my mind off all of that, I started thinking about how I was going to fund this business.

I had been saving up money, but it wasn't nearly enough. I thought about asking my parents for a loan to start up my business. Mom was a realtor, and Dad a criminal attorney, so they had it. I hated the thought of getting a bank loan. My parents were always Michelle's bank, so why wouldn't they be mine too - for once? I hardly ever asked them for anything, anyways.

I saw my vision for my boutique already. I knew how I wanted everything, but I just needed to get my head in the game and make it happen. That's why I didn't need to date. I could hardly stay focused on my own. I knew a man would distract me even more.

Mom and Dad agreed to give me the business loan, but they wanted to be sure I had my shit together before handing over so much money. Again, it was a loan not free money, so if I didn't have my shit together, I had no check. That was easy as hell! I needed those bands, and for it, I was going to do whatever it took.

Asking them was easier than I thought it would be. I decided on opening up a boutique here in Charlotte and hopefully expand my business later on. I was so busy with working at the realtor office and trying to get everything together with my business, I was exhausted. I hadn't talked to Chanel in weeks. I hadn't hung out with my family in weeks. I just needed a break.

The day I decided to call everyone to have a little get-together at my house, Josh called me.

"Hey, Tara, what's up?"

"Oh, hi, Josh. I'm good, just exhausted from dealing with life. How have you been? I haven't seen you since the housewarming."

"I'm good, actually. I was calling to ask you if you wanted to take a trip to the A, my brother, Chris, is having a grand opening for his new club and thought about you rollin' with us, if you had some time. I also have a little surprise for everyone I'm going to reveal."

"Hell yeah! I need that shit! That sounds amazing. Thanks for the invite. Who's on the guest list?"

Josh laughed. "Well, the usual. Same ol' people we always party with. Also, some family and friends. He's opening it up with a partner of his, so I'm sure he will invite people as well. It's gonna be dope!"

"Sounds like it's gon' be lit. I'm definitely there! Just text me the information."

I called Chanel, Michelle, Allie and Gina for us to talk about the trip and how we were all going to get there. We were all excited. I had never been to Atlanta and I hadn't heard or seen Chris since my housewarming. I can't even lie, I was kind of anxious to see him again, but I wasn't telling anyone that; especially, not Chanel.

Us girls decided to ride together. We took turns driving, while the guys rode together. I was ready to get there, get drunk and shake the little piece of ass my momma gave me. Turning up in the A was gon' to be memorable for me!

We arrived at our hotel that night. Allie was good at makeup and beat our faces to the gawds. Chanel had hands with the wand and flat iron, so she tightened our weaves up and got our hair slayed and laid. I styled everybody, making sure our outfits were on point. After getting dolled up, we headed to the club, walking in as a group of bad bitches! We stepped in the club, as if we came to take over that motherfucker!

We met the guys there. Josh was coming a little later than the rest of us. It was a really nice club, better than I had expected. They really put in work, time and lots of money. We had VIP and got in free. We were only responsible for our drinks, which was cool. I could definitely get use to this royal treatment.

"Hey, hey!" We heard a deep voice approaching us. It was Chris and his partner.

"Hey, guys, this is my partner, Andrew. He's from Atlanta and I met him through mutual friends, years ago, we've been buddies ever since," Chris said to us.

He also introduced us individually to Andrew. When he got to me, he started smiling, as he switched his tone up a little bit.

"And this is Tara, we've only met once, but I like her already," he said to Andrew, in front of everyone else.

All I could do was blush. Everyone looked at us and smiled, especially, Chanel. It was silent for a few minutes, which made the moment a bit awkward, and then Josh walked up.

He had this beautiful Dominican girl with him. Young, slim and tall. About mid to late 20s. She had long, jet-black hair and light-brown eyes. She was fine as fuck. Josh had him a bad bitch, no doubt! We all were meeting her for the first time and everyone had their eyes on her. No one had expected to see Josh with a woman like her. He wasn't a bad looking guy. He just dealt with different women, way different from her.

"Wassup, y'all, this is my girl, Gracie. She's from da A and recently started her modeling career out here. This is the surprise I told y'all about," Josh said.

"Hi, nice to meet everyone," Gracie said, in a soft voice.

You could tell she was a shy person. She walked over and sat next to me.

"Come on, guys, let's go grab the beautiful ladies some drinks," Chris said, as the rest of them got up and left.

"Hey, girl, you so fine. What you doing with Josh," Chanel said, bluntly.

I elbowed Chanel in the side, as a sign to chill. I didn't want her to ruin it for them or make Gracie have second thoughts.

Gracie laughed and said, "He's a really sweet guy. We have been dating for about six months now and I really like him."

"Josh is genuinely a good guy, he really is. So, are y'all gonna keep doing the long-distance relationship or one of y'all are going to move," I asked her.

"Well, my family is here, and his family is in North Carolina, so it's just hard for the both of us to decide who's going to make the big move. We are just taking it one day at a time," Gracie said.

"Well, if you decide to move to Charlotte, you will have all of us too. It's like we are your extended family," Michelle said.

Gracie giggled and then said, "I appreciate that."

"What took you so long to come around," Chanel asked.

She was drilling the girl, as if she was being interviewed to get in the military. One question after another. That was Chanel. She was really being herself but easing up a little bit wasn't a bad idea. Damn!

"Well, honestly, I've just been busy; caught up with work and it seemed like no timing was enough timing or good timing for it all to happen. I still haven't met his mom and he's dying for me to meet her. I really want to as well. It's just hard to take off time, when you are new to an industry, a competitive one at that, and trying to take on all opportunities possible," Gracie said.

Gracie replied to Chanel damn good! She made me proud! She wasn't rude, but she showed no sign of weakness either! She would definitely fit into our circle.

"I totally understand, girl," I said.

I really liked this chick. Although, I didn't know her from a can of paint. First impressions always spoke volumes! Her spirit sat right with me, the vibe wasn't off, and just by how she spoke, I could tell she had a good head on her shoulders and took no shit. From that moment on, I knew she was a good person.

The guys walked back with our drinks. Chris handed me mine and asked that he speak with me for a second. I got up and we started chatting. He said he wanted to email me, but he was just busy with work. He told me he would really like to take me out, while I was in Atlanta, and show me around. He even asked that I stay a little longer than everyone else and said my hotel and flight expenses would be on him.

It all sounded good, but I still had my guard up. It was hard for me to trust again. I didn't want my past relationship to affect my happiness and my future, though, so I decided to take him up on his offer and we exchanged numbers this time. I was a little nervous… ok, a lot! I hardly knew the guy, but it was Josh's brother and he seemed cool, so, why not? What's the worst that could happen, right?

Michelle couldn't believe I was staying in an unfamiliar city with a complete stranger. She thought I was insane! She wanted to stay with me, but hell, I wasn't paying for my own expenses so I damn sure wasn't paying for hers and neither was she. Norris was furious, once he heard about it. I didn't understand why he was so jealous about me talking and hanging out with Chris, though. We were over and done with.

He fucked up his chance, he came and left. It was time for him to grow up and move on. I did. But you know what they say, 'You never know what you have until it's gone'. His time expired and he knew that already. I'm thankful that he moved out of the way for a real man to step in and show me how a queen is supposed to be treated.

The next morning, I woke up to so many texts and emails. I had lots of text from Norris that I just ignored. He was still trippin' about the night before and what he saw. Obviously, he didn't want to see me happy and I refused to entertain his nonsense.

I also saw a text from an unsaved number that said, "Good morning, beautiful queen."

It made me blush. I already knew who it was. It had to be Chris.

I texted back, "Good morning, handsome."

Then, I got another text that said, "Oh, how sweet, Tara. Why can't you reply to my text I send off of my phone? Is it like that?"

It was Norris, using someone else's phone from a number I'd never seen before. I was so annoyed! I couldn't believe he was doing so much right now to get my attention. So, I played along and replied back, "Fuck you, don't text me!"

Moments later, I got a "Good morning, beautiful" text, again, from an unsaved number.

At that point, I was over the games, so I replied, "Who the hell is this?!"

They replied back, instantly, and the text read, "It's Chris, sweetheart. I'm sorry! Was I out of line?"

I felt like an asshole! It was early, and I was super annoyed with how my morning was starting. I didn't even want to reply back! I felt like an idiot!

"Oh, I'm sorry. No, it's fine. Good morning," I replied back to Chris.

"Are you ok? Is something wrong," he asked.

I started thinking about what I could say to ease the conversation and for him to forgive how I came off.

"No, I'm ok. Was up early, not a morning person."

"Oh...ok, well get some rest, start over and call me later, I can't wait to spend the day with you!"

He was so sweet, I blushed the entire time I texted him.

"Cool, sounds good... ttyl!" After sending my last message to him, I laid in the bed, rereading our texts, while smiling.

It was all cool until everyone walked in and saw me.

"Ok! So, it's early and your blushing! Tell me, tell me," Chanel said, as she hopped in bed with me. Before I could say anything, Allie grabbed the phone and ran!

I hopped up out the bed, and there I was, running around the hotel room with my thong and t-shirt on. No bra, socks or anything. I'm chasing her, as she's running and looking at the phone, trying to read out loud. Gina walked in the door from getting breakfast downstairs with Norris and Steven!

I didn't care about the phone, at that point, I was damn near naked in front of these assholes! I tried covering up with everything I could grab but it didn't work. Steven just stared, and then once he realized, he turned his head! Norris, on the other hand... totally different story.

It was just what he wanted to see. They all went in different areas, spreading out, trying to give me privacy. Norris stood there, smirking. He already annoyed me first thing in the morning, he hadn't seen me naked in God knows how long and he was currently getting free ass and titty shots!

I finally just got up and walked in the room; Norris followed me. I tried closing the door on him, but he refused. He came in and closed the door behind him. He started kissing on my cheek and rubbing on me. It took me back to that very first night we had sex. The best night ever. He was still the only guy, besides Tommy from college, I had hooked up with. He was still the best I ever had, and quite frankly, I missed him a little bit.

We were kids when we hooked up and we were grown now. He was so experienced and amazing at what he did back then as a kid, I was kind of curious to know what he was like as a man. He still looked good, his body was still toned and well taken care of. I was anxious.

He whispered in my ear, "One last time, I miss you!"

Then, I whispered back, "Make it quick."

He got on top of me and pulled the covers over us. As he kissed on my neck, he rubbed my pussy. Surprised that I still got wet like I used to, he pulled his fingers from underneath the blanket to look at them. He looked at it and I went in, slurping juices off his fingertips. It had been over a year since I had sex. I was ready. He slid on a rubber and started to stick it in. I moaned and moaned! He stroked it about 10 times and then Chanel busted through the door. She screamed and closed it.

Apparently, Norris forgot to lock the door. Thank God we were covered. I pushed him off me. It took everything in me to do that. Once he started, I didn't want to stop. I missed him so much! It was still good, and I was three seconds away from an orgasm. I was so angry that we had to stop. That day started fucked up for me. I was ready to see what Chris had planned for us.

Norris walked out the room and back to his. I went in the shower and sat on the bed for a while after. I couldn't figure out what that was all about! I was totally over Norris! I didn't know what made me do what we did, and then Chanel caught us. Better her than anyone else, though. I could convince Chanel to keep her mouth shut, not so much with any of the other girls.

I just hoped Norris didn't tell Josh, because Josh may tell Chris, and that could really fuck it up for us before it even started. I was so paranoid! I even thought about cancelling with Chris. It would be too weird to be around him, after I just somewhat fucked his brother's best friend - again! Not only that, it was right before meeting up with him.

I called Chanel in the room.

"What the fuck just happened with y'all two? You know what, don't even tell me! I don't wanna know," Chanel yelled!

"Shhh... be quiet! It was an accident, ok! It will never happen again! I just need you to forget what just happened and keep your mouth shut! I don't want this to get out and ruin what me and Chris could potentially have! Can you promise me? Promise me you will never mention this, Chanel," I whispered.

Chanel rolled her eyes and then said, "You know I won't!"

I hugged her and kissed her on the cheek!

"Oh no, don't kiss me! I don't know where your mouth been," she said. We both laughed, and she walked out the room.

They all began to pack up to leave. I started packing as well. Chris was getting me a different hotel room. A "luxury, queen suite" as he called it. He knew we weren't sleeping together and he was totally fine with that. I called him, and he came to pick me up. We went to the hotel he booked first, so I could drop off my things. It was the best room I had ever seen. It had a nice, Downtown view, a jacuzzi, walk-in shower, pool table, and even a dancing pole. I had never been on a pole before, but since I was going to be in this big-ass room alone, why not get on it, shake some ass and learn some tricks?

He showed me where he stayed. He was in a condo as well, but nothing like mine. It was so much better and elegant! He also drove nice cars. He had a Ferrari and a Mercedes. I wanted to just move my things right on in. He showed me around Atlanta, we went out to eat, as we talked and got to know each other more.

He was a single, 27-year-old man and I was 25. He had no kids and had never been to jail. He didn't graduate high school but still made a way for himself and became successful. He'd never been married. He likes to travel, work, and spend time with his family and friends. We actually had a lot in common. I liked him before but was not interested in being more than business partners or friends. After spending the day with him, he had won me over. Getting to know who he was outside of "Josh's brother" and a club owner, made me like him even more. It was how he acted, his personality, his mentality, his voice and everything else. He was a really attractive guy too.

Dark-skinned, slim, toned, about 6'3" and I'm 5'9," so I needed a tall guy. Chris had tattoos all over and a pretty smile. He was even a little older - like I liked it. I never told him I wanted him. I took things slowly. I wanted him to make the move on me.

When it was time for me to leave him and go back to Charlotte, he went to the airport with me and sat with me until it was time for my flight. We laughed and talked to pass time. He repeatedly said how much he enjoyed spending time with me, how he didn't want me to leave and wished that he could be with me forever. I promised him that we would meet up again soon. He gave me a hug and held me.

When I got home, I thought about the Atlanta trip from start to finish and how Norris acted the entire time. I decided to reach out to him. I texted him. At first, I was hesitant about it, but I was dying to know what that was all about.

I waited on Norris to reply. About 30 minutes later, he texted back and asked if I was home. I told him yes, but then he didn't respond back. About an hour later, as I was dozing off to sleep, I heard the doorbell ring. I looked through the peephole and it was Norris. I stood there for a minute and then I opened the door.

"What are you doing here unannounced," I asked.

"Why text, when we can talk in person," Norris responded.

"You can't be doing that! What if I had company?"

"What if you had company," Norris said, as he walked in the living room, laid across the couch, making himself comfortable.

"Do you want me to leave?"

Well, yeah, but no, I thought in my head. I stood there, silently, and said, "Well, you're here now."

"Did I ever tell you this was a nice place? I know I was drunk the night of the housewarming, so I can't remember."

"Well, if you did, I can't remember. I was just as drunk as you," I said, grinning.

"You looked nice in Atlanta, by the way!"

"Well, thank you! Speaking of Atlanta, what was that all about? You seemed a little jealous from the attention Chris showed me."

"Oh, no, I was just drunk. I want you to be happy. He's a cool dude and all, but he ain't me!"

I just blushed, uncontrollably, and rolled my eyes.

He asked if we could watch a movie. He ordered some pizza and wings for us, while we laid down, watching a movie. We ended up in the room because the bed was more comfortable than the couch.

Chapter 8

"Vulnerable Woman"

As he came underneath the covers, he eased up behind me, holding me, while resting his head on mine.

"I missed you so much! This is where we were supposed to be! Together, in our own home. Only thing we're missing is our little baby next to us," Norris whispered in my ear.

Him bringing that back up brought tears to my eyes. Reminiscing on the past brought back anger towards him I didn't know I still had.

"Look at me," Norris said.

I tried to wipe my eyes dry, before turning, but as I turned, tears continued to drop.

"Why are you crying, baby," he asked me, in a sincere voice.

"I was just thinkin'!"

"About the baby," he asked.

I shook my head yes, while wiping my eyes more.

"We have our whole lives to make it happen again. We gon' be alright. It will happen again," Norris said, as he kissed me on my lips.

I closed my eyes and kissed him back. Rubbing my hands all over his body, as I thought about Chris. Then, I stopped. I couldn't go on.

I sat up in the bed and said, "I can't do this, Norris!"

"Why not, baby? Huh?"

He continued to kiss on me. My cheeks. My neck and all over my body. He started rubbing on my clit, trying but not really trying to move his hands off me. He pushed me down on the bed, threw my legs in the air and shoved his face in my pussy. Grabbing on his head, snatching on the sheets, scratching the headboard and shaking like I was going to have a seizure, I moaned loudly. Within minutes, I came in his mouth.

I couldn't resist. I still loved Norris. I never wanted us to end. He gave me the best sex I'd ever had. There was no way in hell I could turn back now. He came up, looked at me in my eyes, as he rubbed on himself, rushing to unbuckle his pants.

"You miss Daddy," he asked, before I sucked my cum off his face.

"Mmhmm," I responded, quickly.

It wasn't until after we both came and went two rounds before I realized we never used a condom. I laid in the bed on my back, looking at the ceiling. He tried cuddling after, but as I started thinking, I threw his hands off me. I couldn't believe I was so stupid. In the heat of the moment, and worried about my orgasm, I wasn't thinking clearly.

I got up and went to the bathroom. I stood in the mirror lookin' at my reflection.

"How could you be so dumb," I asked myself. "How?" I went on, as if I was getting an answer! I hopped in the shower and cried heavily, scrubbing my body as hard as I could in disgust. When I got out, Norris was asleep.

"Get up! Get up, Norris," I yelled, as I tried shaking him.

"What's wrong, Tara?"

"You, nigga, I need you to go!"

"Damn, is it like that?"

"Hell yeah!"

"Can I call you tomorrow?"

"NO," I responded, slamming the door behind him.

I stood with my back against the door, thinking about the shit I'd done. Worried, Disgusted and Terrified. As I stood in the kitchen, my phone started ringing. It scared the hell out of me! It was Chris. I didn't want to talk to him, after what just happened with Norris and I. It would be awkward, but I answered anyways.

We talked for a while. I was trying to keep my cool and act as normal as possible. He told me how much he missed me and that he was coming to town. He wanted to see me when he came, but he never told me when he was coming. I wanted to see him too, so I agreed to it. I was starting to like him a little bit; ok, a lot!

A few days later, Chanel texted me to check on me. We hadn't spoken in a while and that was unusual. She wanted to meet up for dinner, but I told her I was too tired. I just wanted to be alone. I had a lot of shit on my mind. I sat in the house, watched some TV and tried getting some work done, as I had plans to meet with my parents the next day.

The next day, I woke up late in the day. I got up about two hours before my parents and I's lunch date and woke up to damn near 50 missed calls. All of them were from Michelle. She never called me like that, so I knew at that moment something was wrong. I hopped up and called her back, immediately! When I called back, she was in tears.

"Calm down, Michelle. What's wrong," I asked her.

She sat on the phone, speechless. I repeatedly asked her what was wrong.

"Michelle! Speak to me!" I was anxious to know what was going on and I was beyond worried. It was killing me that she wasn't saying anything.

I needed to know, but she never spoke, so I hung up. I called Mom. She didn't answer. I called Dad. He didn't answer. I ended up calling Michelle back.

"Michelle, please, I'm begging you! Tell me what's wrong!"

She stuttered terribly, while she sobbed heavily. It was so bad that I could hardly understand her. I did catch on when she said Mom and Dad had been in a car accident and they were gone.

I dropped my phone and stood there. I started crying heavily! I could not believe what I heard! That was the worst news I had ever gotten in my life. I didn't know what to think! I was broken and there was no fixing me! I stood there in disbelief, as I cried. Michelle was still on the phone, but I left it on the floor. I didn't want to hear anything else. My mom...My dad...Gone forever! I couldn't process that. There was no way in hell that shit was real.

I cried for hours. I didn't touch my phone, I didn't even move from the spot that I was originally in when I found out. After about three hours, I called Michelle back.

"Where are you," I asked her.

She told me she was home, she needed to leave the hospital because it was too depressing. I wanted to go see them, though, so I asked that she go back to the hospital with me. She didn't want to, but for me, she did. I went to pick her up and we rode over together. As we walked through the hospital, my hands started shaking, my mouth started to water, and I started to feel faint.

"Michelle, I'm getting lightheaded. I'm not sure I can go through with this," I told her.

Michelle grabbed me by the arm and stopped me in the hallway. She looked at me and said, "We're here already, Tara. What do you want to do? I don't need you passing out on me, it's enough going on. Can you really handle this? Let me just be honest, it is hard."

I put my head down, indecisive about if I wanted to go through with it or not. Michelle lifted my chin and said, "Come on, sis, you can do it. If you don't, I know you will regret it. Let's go. I got you."

We walked in the cold room, and as I got closer to them, I got weaker. When I stood next to them, my body got numb; and as I continued to look them in their faces, a part of me died more on the inside. It wasn't fair! It wasn't right! It was unbelievable! How could this be?

We were at the hospital for an hour. Finally, we got the word on what happened. They were hit by teenagers, on their way to a church meeting, before our brunch date. Emergency officials tried rushing them to the hospital, but they died from head trauma and internal bleeding. It was nothing they could really do. It was too late.

When we left the hospital, we went back to my condo… The two of us. I called Chanel over and told her the news then. Grieving and trying to cope with everything, together. It was killing me to know that my parents were never coming back.

They left. Then, an hour later, I got a knock on the door. I wasn't expecting anyone else. I asked who it was, but they didn't answer. When I looked through the peephole, all I saw was flowers. I was thinking, *ok, maybe someone was sending flowers on my parents' behalf,* so I opened the door.

When I opened the door, it was Chris. He had flowers in his hand, some Japanese takeout, some candy and a Redbox movie. I wasn't up for a movie night, nor company, after what just happened. On the other hand, the man was putting in effort to comfort and support me in a time of need, so I couldn't just turn him down and send him home. I put on a fake smile - the best that I could - and welcomed him in.

"I don't mean to sound rude and all, but what are you doing here," I asked Chris.

"I heard about what happened, I wasn't able to make it earlier, so I thought I would come by, as I promised. I know you have a lot going on and I just wanted to be here for you! But if you want me to leave, I understand," Chris replied.

"No, no! It's ok. Make yourself comfortable." I welcomed him.

He handed me the flowers and candy and then held up the takeout and movie. He said, "Hope you're hungry and up for a movie."

"Wow, this is sweet. The flowers are beautiful. How did you know I liked Japanese," I asked him.

"Well, Chanel told me. I kind of went behind your back and got some information on you from your best friend. I needed to find out a good way of surprising you, without asking you, so I went to the closest person to you. I hope you're not mad."

I giggled, lightly, then replied, "No, it's cool. You definitely get points for effort."

He winked at me and smiled. In the back of my mind, I wondered how they contacted one another, but I knew Chanel wouldn't do no dirty shit to me, so I didn't put too much thought into it.

"So, my queen, are you hungry," Chris yelled to me, as he stood in the kitchen.

"I'm not, actually! I don't have an appetite... I'm sorry!"

"When was the last time you ate? You cannot go without eating," he fussed.

"I ate a little earlier, I'll be fine," I said to him, as I smiled.

Chris and I didn't really have a chance to talk. He was calling and texting me, but I wasn't responding. I had a lot going on. So, we used that alone time to our advantage.

He put his food down and hugged me. He kissed me over and over again on the forehead and told me how much he was here for me and that he wanted to help in any way possible. We got to talk, and I opened up about everything and how I felt. I broke completely down.

I was a little embarrassed, but it also showed me how sympathetic and caring he really was. He said all the right things and comforted me as my mom did. I swear it was something about this guy that I just couldn't get enough of. He had to be heaven-sent.

He told me that he wanted to stay the week with me and that he wasn't leaving until he knew that I was ok. He spoke sternly when he said that too. He mentioned getting a hotel close by and coming by every day. I told him there was no need to spend money on a hotel when I have a big condo all to myself. It was more than enough room for him. I loved being around him. I was hoping his company would help take my mind off things.

When he got up to put his food away, he told me he was running to the car and he would be back up in a second. When he came back, he had a bag, but he went straight in the bathroom. I found that a bit strange, but I just sat there and minded my business. I didn't want to invade the man's privacy so soon.

He was in the bathroom for about five minutes before I started to hear the water in the tub running. I started questioning what the hell was really going on. I had never seen a grown-ass man take a bath. It was very awkward and a bit of a turn off, to be honest, until I got up and went to see what the deal was. The bathroom door was open, so I walked straight in. When I walked in, I couldn't believe my eyes.

I immediately noticed the lavender aroma that filled the bathroom and lingered into my room. He had a bubble bath running for me with real rose petals in it. Candles were lit around the tub and massage oil was on the counter. It was so cute and just what I needed. He even had a bath pillow in there. I was a sucker for shit like that. When I walked in, he was leaning over the tub to turn the water off. When he turned around, I caught him by surprise.

"So, what do you think," he asked me.

"I love it," I said, as my eyes watered.

He came and hugged me and told me there was no need to cry and that the little setup he did was nothing compared to what he had in store for me. I wasn't a materialistic kind of chick, but it was nice to see how much a man really likes and appreciates the person you are, without having to give up some ass first. Damn, I could get used to this.

After being in the tub for about 15 minutes, I called for him to come in the bathroom with me. Not in the tub, but I just needed his presence. He came in, put the toilet seat down and just sat on the toilet, as we talked.

Shortly after talking, it got silent. He started to sweat and didn't seem like himself. He was starting to scare me. Concerned, I stared at him for a while, and then he started speaking. He told me he wanted to ask me something, but he didn't know if it was a good time. I told him right then and there, if he was going to be in my life, even as a friend, he had to promise to be completely honest with what we talked about and to never hold anything from me. He promised and hesitantly started speaking.

"You know how I called you my queen, right? Well, I really want you to be that. I want you all to myself. I love everything about you. I want to take it to the next level, but I don't want to overstep any boundaries as a friend, being that I'm really feeling you. I want you to officially be my queen and only mine!"

I couldn't believe what I was hearing. One reason was because my mother and father had just passed away hours ago. Why now? Couldn't this wait? The other reason was because I'd been wanting to hear that for a while now; before all of this happened. I knew I said I wanted to take it slow, but I really wanted him. How slow can a girl really take it, when a fine-ass nigga made her feel like the queen she had never felt like before?

Besides, if I took it too slow, another bitch had chances to take my place, and I refused for that to happen. I played it cool and said, "I would love to be your queen, but only if you promise to be my king only."

"That's easy! I promise, beautiful," he said, right before kissing me.

"You don't know how happy you make me. I've never dated a girl like you. You're young but wise; baby girl, you just different," he continued.

I was overjoyed to hear those words come out his mouth. At that point, I felt like I had found me a real man.

When I got out the bathtub, he wrapped me in a towel, and he massaged my body from head to toe. Again, I'd never been rubbed like that before. His hands were so soft, he applied just enough pressure in all the right places. The warmth from his hands touching my body felt so good, it started to make me horny. After he finished massaging me, I got on top of him and started kissing all over his face, neck and chest. While I was on top, he continued to rub on my body some more. I could tell he was into everything I was doing to him.

He got up, and as he kissed me, he flipped me over with one arm. He was very masculine, and it turned me on how he did it. He was on top of me, kissing all over me. He started pulling his pants and boxers off, but then he stopped. I was in the mood and ready to see what he was working with. Now, I'm like, *why in the hell would you stop?*

He lifted up, looked me in my eyes and asked me, "Do you really want to do this right now?"

I told him, "Hell yeah!" and pulled him down on me.

"Are you sure," he asked, again!

"I repeated, "Hell yeah! I'm all yours! Now, give it to me!"

He looked in my eyes for about five seconds, while smiling, and then went on.

He ripped open the condom with his teeth, put it on and slid it in. When I tell you I was breathless, I really was. I couldn't breathe! I started to question if I really could handle it. He was only going in and I started to run. It was huge! Yes, bigger than Norris - without a doubt! What the hell was going on? How was I finding these big dick men? It wasn't on purpose. I was definitely keeping him! There's no way anybody else was fucking him (I know, I know! I said that about Norris, back in the day, but how Chris made me feel, anybody could have Norris.)!

I moaned, I screamed, I ran! And guess what? He never stopped! He was determined to pleasure me the best way possible. He gave me him! All of him!

A part of me couldn't believe we were doing it, in that moment, but I couldn't stop him. Not that I really wanted to. I started to feel bad about fucking Norris days prior, but that was before Chris and I made it official, so I brushed it off and worried less. I was off all week, Chris would be here with me all week, and we were definitely fucking every day until he left. I needed some distraction from reality, anyways; although, I knew I still had to face it.

When we stopped, we went for round 2, then round 3, and even round 4. He was like the Energizer Bunny! He kept on going, as if it was still the first round! It seemed like he never got tired. I was! I was exhausted! But I wanted more, and more and more. I craved his loving. I needed it! I wanted it, as much as he wanted to give it to me.

After hours of going at it, we finally stopped. Realizing we couldn't find the condom on the last go 'round, we panicked. We looked on the bed, Chris checked my pussy, and then we looked on the floor and there it was, popped wide open, just as my pussy felt. I worried myself about when the condom popped. I was dealing with enough. I was stressing heavily, and that was just another thing to wreck my brain about.

I woke up pretty late the next day. Chris got up before me. When I opened my eyes, he was standing in his boxers, looking fine as fuck. A whole lot of chocolate stood there with tattoos all over his body. He even oiled himself. He looked edible! He was holding breakfast in his hands. He was such a gentleman, doing all the things for me I had never experienced before.

He came over to me, kissed me on my cheek and said, "Good morning, beautiful! I hope you woke up with an appetite."

I blushed hard. That was all I could do. I was so appreciative of him, and to have him here with me. He made dealing with the death of my parents much easier. He showed me so much more than I'd ever been shown before. I was convinced, at that point, that I was dealing with nothing but bustas before him.

He had golden brown pancakes, crispy bacon, and soft, fluffy eggs on the plate, with a side of ice-cold orange juice. It was funny how he knew so much about my likes and dislikes so soon.

It had to be Chanel, again, who told him what I liked. I must say, when Chanel is involved, I'm never disappointed. She made sure guys were up to my standards and knew all that they needed to know to make me happy.

I started to eat, but then he refused for me to feed myself. He insisted on feeding me, instead. We sat in the room, watching TV, as he fed me, and then we heard a knock at the door. I lifted up to go get it, but Chris told me to stay put. He grabbed a pair of pants to put on and headed to the door.

As he walked to the door, I just prayed it wasn't Norris. How awkward would that be? I needed no drama. I peeped through my cracked room door, as Chris approached the door. I was nervous, so nervous I was shaking. Norris popped up unannounced just days ago and saw no wrong in it. I knew, almost 100%, that it was Norris. If it was Norris, I wouldn't know what to do or say to him.

The door opened, and I heard Chanel's voice! I could breathe again. Thank God it was her and only her. But then I started thinking. What in the hell was she doing here? Why did she show up and not call first? Why did people think it was ok to pop up at my house unannounced? I told her, "Just a minute." I needed to get dressed. I still needed to take a shower, but I threw on some clothes because she would be quick.

Before I could get dressed completely, she busted in the room!

"Not like I've never seen you naked before," she hollered.

"Uh… privacy," I replied.

"No best friend allows their best friend privacy… girl, please," she said, while rolling her eyes.

Chris walked in behind her, shrugging his shoulders, and said, "I have nothing to do with this, I'm staying out of it. Oh yeah, baby, I'ma give y'all some time; call me when you get up and going. I'll be at Josh's." He kissed me on the cheek, grabbed a shirt and left.

Chanel looked at Chris, as he walked out, and then looked back at me, and then looked in Chris' direction again.

"Oh, boy, here comes your million and one questions," I said to her, giggling.

"So, for someone who wants to take it slow, you sure is moving fast," Chanel said, as she looked around.

"Looks like the guy practically moved on in."

"He's just here to comfort me while all of this is going on. He's in town for about a week and I told him he could stay here, instead of getting a hotel. I'm in this big-ass place alone, anyways. I could use some company to help get my mind off things."

"Sooo...is it working," Chanel asked, smirking.

I started blushing and said, "Um… yeah!"

"So, are y'all like, officially dating or are y'all still friends," Chanel questioned.

"Well, it's funny that you asked that because last night he popped up when y'all left. He brought flowers and candy and he ran me a romantic bubble bath, and while I was relaxing, he came in and told me he wanted to ask me something. He was like, 'I really like you and I want you to be mine.' I was shocked I didn't know what to say."

"Well, please tell me you said yes, bitch, because he is fine! If you don't want him, I'll take him!"

I looked at her sideways, in a jealous way, and said, "Bitch, he's mine," in a firm voice!

I didn't go into detail about our sex last night. I thought I would keep it to myself. She already seemed too interested already! I didn't want to give her any ideas. Some things you just don't tell anyone. Not even your close family and friends.

Chapter 9

"Filling the Holes in My Heart"

I got washed up and dressed, while Chanel ate the leftovers Chris cooked. I could hear her from the kitchen, as she smacked on pancakes. "Not only is he fine but he can cook too. You better keep him!" I just rolled my eyes. I didn't even respond. I didn't know what was getting into me. I've never been the jealous type, but for some odd reason, the comments Chanel was making about Chris really bothered me. I never mentioned it to her, though. We had so much going on with the funeral, I just brushed it off, played it cool and went on about my day.

The funeral had come and gone. It turned out nice. Everyone showed, and it really felt like a celebration. A few days later, Michelle and I sat down with the lawyer, as we both were the only, living beneficiaries left. They had it in their wills that Michelle and I get everything they owned. We were the only kids, so they pretty much left everything 50/50 for us.

We had to split everything. We really didn't want to sell the house, it was our childhood home, and they kept it well, but we had to. It was a $250,000 house that we could not - at the time - afford to keep up with, so selling it was our only option. Michelle took a car and I actually gave Chanel the other. My mom loved her like her own, so Michelle and I agreed to count her in.

I made a promise to her many years ago, if I had it, I would make sure that she did too, and that's exactly what I did.

Together, in the bank, they had over $200,000, so Michelle and I split it in the middle. I didn't know what she had planned to do with her money, but I knew where mine was going, and I had no doubts about it. Michelle was very materialistic and irresponsible, so I knew for sure she would blow hers on bullshit and that's what she did.

Yes, here I was, 25 with over $200,000 in my account from splitting the money in the bank and the money from the house, but that didn't make me happy! Realizing that my dad wouldn't be able to walk me down the aisle and my mom wasn't here to help pick out my wedding dress really hurt me. Neither one of them would be here to meet my future husband and kids. They wouldn't be here to witness my success, and I won't be able to see the looks on their faces when they saw how well put together my business was. It hurt. I didn't care about the money!

Michelle and I grew closer after their death. We spent more time together, we talked more, and I actually enjoyed it, although she was even more stuck-up and much more of a snobby bitch with all that money, than she was before. I was used to it and realized it would never change.

She took the tragedy harder than I did, though. I think she tried to cope with it by partying and drinking and that bothered me. It scared me. She was all I had left, and there was no way in hell I was losing her too.

I begged her for months to slow down, but she was always in denial about how much she drank. I was a little relieved to know that she had her girls in the house with her to keep an eye out, but sometimes, I thought they influenced her to do it too. Michelle was a grown-ass woman. I had a life of my own. Although I loved and cared about her, I could not babysit her.

Chris was still by my side. We were going stronger than before. Four and a half months had passed, and during that time, I learned so much more about who he was. Especially, during the time after the accident. He was Prince Charming! The best guy I had ever dated. I couldn't see myself without him. I believed in my heart he was the best it could get. He stayed in Charlotte more. I quit my job at the real estate office where Mom and I both worked, and he helped me to become my own boss.

I didn't have a job, I was living off the money I had to make ends meet, while getting my boutique together and ready to open. I still resided in my condo to save some money, but I had plans on buying a home soon. I went to Atlanta with Chris more and things were really good between us.

Gracie became my other best friend and we started talking more. I loved hanging out with her, when I went to the A. I appreciated her showing up for me after the accident, when we hardly knew each other. That showed a lot! Josh was pretty damn happy to know Gracie had somebody to chill with. She didn't know many people here, so she hesitated on coming the majority of the time. For some reason, I think he used me to get her here.

Gracie was still modeling and quite successful. She was so good at what she did. She looked good doing it and her body was banging. She had it all together. She travelled a lot, and being that I wasn't employed, she invited me to a lot of her gigs. I supported her, as I always did. She was a really cool chick and I fucked with boss bitches.

Chris was in town and told me he wanted to do dinner. It was a surprise, so all I needed to do was get dressed and he would pick me up. I got dressed, and by the time I was done, he was downstairs, standing outside the car, holding roses in his hand. He kissed and hugged me. He also complimented me, as he always did. He opened the car door, handed me my roses and blindfolded me.

He'd never done this before. The guy was full of surprises, ok? It never got old and I got used to it. I was one lucky woman to be able to call him mine. Every moment with him was enjoyable and he kept a smile on my face.

Four months in, he was still doing the most for me, even after getting the cat. Normally after you gave it up, these niggas would stop putting in effort, but not this one. That's how I knew he was different. He was a keeper!

We pulled up to this bougie and expensive-looking restaurant. It definitely wasn't the Applebee's that Norris' cheap-ass took me to. We walked in there and was seated immediately, as our reservations were already made. The place was beautiful. Chandeliers hung from the ceiling. The tables were nicely-decorated with wrinkle-free table cloths. Bottles of champagne sat on the tables, along with fresh flowers and rose petals, per request. Each table had a waiter or waitress of their own that stood by our side the entire night. It was a five-star, top-notch restaurant.

After ordering our food, it showed up in maybe 10 minutes and it was steaming hot. I was impressed! I wasn't expecting to get the food so soon, as the place was packed. I felt like I was really living it up. He always made me feel like the queen he always called me.

The night was going well. We were laughing and talking, just enjoying ourselves. While I ate my mashed potatoes and steak, I started to feel nauseous. I got up and ran to the bathroom.

Chris followed me, yelling, "Baby, wait!"

I was in the bathroom for maybe six minutes, vomiting and cleaning myself. When I was done, I walked out the bathroom and Chris was standing outside the door.

"Baby? Are you ok?"

"I don't know what that was about. I just don't feel good. I hate to ruin all of this. You took time putting it all together, but let's just take our food to-go and enjoy it at the house."

He was not upset at all. He was very understanding, actually, and more concerned about why I got sick all of a sudden. We got our food to-go, and on the way home, he checked on me constantly. I just wanted to lie down in bed. I didn't know what was going on.

When we got to the house, after being in there for about ten minutes, I went running to the bathroom, again. I started thinking, what could possibly be causing it. Maybe it was food poisoning. That's what I believed it was and I stuck to it. I texted Chanel, Michelle and Gracie what happened. All of their responses were the same - that I was pregnant.

There was no way I could be pregnant. Well, kind of, but I wasn't ready to go through that again. I didn't want to believe that. Chris asked me if I wanted him to run out and get a test, but I told him no.

I think in the back of his mind he felt like I was pregnant too. We both had businesses to run. We were busy-ass people. Neither one of us had time for a kid. I was still dealing with the abortion I never mentioned to him. I was still grieving over my parents; and although it had been four months, I was still stressing as though it happened yesterday. Being pregnant at that moment was not an option!

Chris laid by me all that night, until I fell asleep. He had work the next day, so he was leaving early in the morning. Once he left, I called my girls to come over.

Luckily, Gracie was in town, so she showed up too. Michelle, Chanel and Gracie came over about 11am. Michelle came with my favorite breakfast, IHOP. Gracie came with some get well balloons and a card. Crazy Chanel showed up with a pregnancy test. Leave it up to her ass to be extra.

It felt good to have them there. Chris was the topic of the conversation, of course. Noticing how happy he made me, they were dying to know if I was pregnant with his baby. Since they insisted, and I knew it was food poisoning, I went in the bathroom and took the damn test. Sure enough, it was positive.

I dropped on the floor and they all came running in.

"I can't believe this," I said, sobbing.

"I don't want to tell anyone!" I continued.

"You don't have to tell anyone, but you have to tell Chris," Gracie said.

"Yeah, she's right," Michelle agreed.

"But we've only been together for four months, how do you think he is going to feel about this? What if it ruins what we've built thus far? What if he dumps me, leaving me with a baby alone? I'm not ready to be a mom, let alone a single one," I cried.

"Honestly, Tara, I think Chris will be excited and just as supportive as he was for everything else you went through. I don't think he is that type of guy! He's madly in love with you! I'm sure he will be delighted to hear this news," Gracie said.

"If he is a real dickhead about it, we know where he be. We can pull up on his ass, fuck him up, flat his tires and ruin all his shit," Chanel chimed in. I giggled, slightly.

"I've got nothing to lose, you know I will," Chanel went on.

"Well, I do, I'm not wit' it," Michelle said.

Then, Gracie said, "Shit, I agree!"

We all laughed, as they lifted me off the floor.

"It's going to be ok. I bet he will be happy! Just watch," Michelle said.

"He better be," Chanel mumbled.

"Well, I guess that explains it," Michelle said.

"Yeah, I guess it do," I said, sniffling.

"Well, how are you.... when are you going to tell him?" Gracie asked.

"Let's send him a picture of the test," Chanel burst out.

"That's so damn ghetto, Chanel," I said.

She took my phone and ran to the bathroom to snap a picture. She sent it to Chris, and less than a minute later, he called. I was nervous as hell! I wasn't ready to talk about it.

My phone rang three times and then he hung up. I was relieved, but then he called back, again and again! On the 4th call, I finally answered and put him on speaker.

"Why didn't you pick up, baby," Chris asked.

"This is the first call I got from you," I lied.

"You know how my service can be at times," I continued.

"Yeah," Chris said, as if he didn't believe me.

"So, you took a pregnancy test?"

"Um...yeah," I said, hesitantly.

"And?"

"I'm...I'm pregnant!"

The phone went silent and I got scared. I knew it wasn't time.

"Baby? Baby are you serious?"

As he asked, I realized that I had never heard him speak in that voice before. Then, I heard him sniffling.

"I'm flying home now, baby! I can't believe we are having a baby! Yes! I'm coming back home," Chris said, excitedly.

"You don't have to leave to come home! You're already there; go 'head and handle what you need to do, I'll be fine," I said, but then Chris cut me off.

"See you in a few hours. I love you!"

Soon as I hung up, Chanel, Michelle and Gracie jumped all over me, screaming.

"I told you," Gracie said.

"But I can't believe he was crying though," Chanel said.

"I'm going be an auntie, I'm going to be an auntie!" Michelle sung.

Then, Chanel and Gracie chimed in on Michelle's song that they ran around my condo singing.

All I could do was laugh at those three fools. They really made it easy! I can't even lie, even though I was stressed about everything, I was starting to feel good. Being pregnant that go 'round was much better than the first time. Everything with Chris was better than the first time. I began to get a little bit more excited.

I went to my first doctor's appointment and Chris was next to me. He loved looking at the ultrasound and hearing the heartbeat. They told me I was about four months along. I couldn't believe I went that long without knowing. That meant I conceived around the time my parents passed away. I was scared as hell. Around that time was right after I came from Atlanta.

I wanted to tell Chris everything from start to finish, but I didn't have it in me to do it. I couldn't. Everything was happening so fast. It was so much we needed to talk about and learn about each other. The last thing I wanted to do was hurt him and ruin the moment.

I started stressing more and more about everything. I had so much on my plate. My girls knew I was out of it, so they put together a dinner date for me at a soul food restaurant, which included the four of us; Michelle, Gracie, Chanel and myself.

I hardly ate my dinner. I picked over most of it. Which led to Gracie asking me what was wrong. They could see it on my face, so I took that moment to spill out everything. I told them what happened in the Atlanta hotel room, but Chanel knew already. Then, I told them about when I got back from Atlanta and what happened in the condo with Norris and me. I did not leave out the part when he didn't use protection either. I continued on about the part when Chris and I fucked like animals almost all week after that. Last but not least, I told them about my doctor's appointment and how I conceived around the time all of that happened.

My life was like a Lifetime movie. After I told them, they all just stared at me. Big-eyed with dropped jaws. They were so shocked! I felt like a damn slut, and in shame, I put my head down. Once I did that, they snapped out of it and started speaking.

"Well, girl, I don't know what to tell ya," Chanel's blabbermouth said.

Gracie chimed in and said to Chanel, "Just chill sometimes, damn! She don't need your bullshit right now, for real!"

"Who is this bougie bitch playing wit'," Chanel hollered

Chanel hopped up at the table so fast and was going in to grab Gracie, but Michelle jumped up, stopped her and stood between them both. I couldn't believe Chanel. She was really trippin'.

"I'll dismiss myself. Call me when you don't have company," Chanel said to me, as she snatched her purse and walked out of the restaurant.

As the months went by, Chanel came around, but she was still distant. I still didn't know what raged her to act out at the dinner. With all the shit I had going on, I didn't have much time to talk about it either.

On the day of my birthday, Chanel showed up at the house. Chris was still at the house and they both told me that she was going to take me shopping for my birthday. I wasn't expecting that, and I didn't know when or even how they were able to put it together, but I rolled with the flow.

I got dressed in the store, after purchasing my items, and then she drove me to a nice banquet hall. It was one I'd seen before, while driving past, always saying how nice it was and how I wondered what the inside looked like, but that day I found out. It was crowded. When I walked in, everyone yelled, "Surprise!" Not only was it a birthday party for me, but a baby shower as well.

As everybody was leaving, I smiled, hugged and thanked everyone. The night went smoothly, until I saw Norris. I started thinking, *well who the fuck invited him and why didn't I get the memo*? I called the girls over and whispered to them.

"Why didn't y'all tell me jackass was coming?"

Everybody seemed clueless of who I was talking about. Then, I continued on, "that jackass," as I pointed at Norris.

Nobody knew he was coming, not even Chanel. I found that a bit strange, though, because they were two peas in a pod, they told each other everything.

Michelle, Chanel and Gracie left from by me, and as I struggled to get up from my seat, I felt soft hands on my back. I knew for sure it was Chris, he always came on time.

"Thank you, honey," I said, as I turned in his direction, smiling. I immediately stopped smiling and stopped in my tracks because it wasn't Chris, it was Norris.

I didn't want to make a scene by telling him what I really wanted to say and acting out, so I just went along with it with a mugged look on my face. He leaned into me and whispered in my ear, "You look very beautiful pregnant, baby. I can't wait to meet my prince or princess," as he rubbed on my belly.

I smiled and whispered back to him, "Get the fuck off of me! I wouldn't have a baby with your ass to save my fuckin' life," then I wobbled off.

Norris was very manipulative, and that was one reason why it was so hard for me to really get over him. I knew he was just trying to ruin my happiness. I wasn't going to let him get to me, though. He was really overstepping boundaries! His pop-ups were never acceptable, but it was getting out of hand.

A week after the baby shower, I went into labor. Luckily, I was home, lying in the bed with Michelle over. Michelle rushed me to the hospital, and she called Chris to meet us there. It was a long, painful process, but worth everything I went through. We welcomed our first kid, a girl, we named Armani. Everyone was there to help celebrate the special moment with us. The room was so full, no one could hardly move.

In the presence of everyone, Chris got on his knees and proposed to me! My hormones were still out of whack and I got extremely emotional! That was something I least expected. I was enjoying the moment I finally got to meet my precious kid and now the man of my dreams, my king, my lover asked me to be his wife! Everything was moving so fast with Chris and I, but I refused to slow it down.

When I saw him on one knee, looking me in my eyes, spilling his heart out to me in front of all those people with that big-ass diamond ring, tears immediately filled my eyes. With no hesitation, I said yes! It was the last place I thought my proposal would happen, but it was still special to me.

Chapter 10

"Forgiving"

The past year was good to my family and I. Motherhood was going great. Our little girl was so adorable. I never knew being a mom would be the best thing that ever happened to me. I never knew I could love someone so much that I'd only known for a year.

After I had Armani, Chris and I waited until she was two months old to get married. It wasn't anything extravagant; we went to the courthouse. With us being new parents and having businesses, there was no time in our agenda to plan a huge wedding like I really wanted. Besides, we didn't want to wait all that time to do so, anyways.

A huge wedding wasn't in the budget either. We bought our first home together, shortly after we married. It was a nice home that had four bedrooms, two and a half baths, a big, beautiful kitchen with an island like I always wanted, and a two-car garage. It was only the three of us, but a beginner home wasn't an option for me. I wanted what I wanted, and I got just that.

The boutique was finally up and running and business was booming. It was busier than I would have ever imagined it to be in the first year. I couldn't have done it without my family, though. Chanel and Michelle were doing good at the shop as my managers. They helped take a lot off of my shoulders, which gave me more time to focus on my household. Chris was busy with his club and his business was getting busier as well.

He left often, as business picked up more. Although I missed him, I got use to him leaving frequently, even though I didn't want to. That left me in Charlotte to raise a kid alone the majority of the time.

I had a sitter for Armani, which helped me tremendously. With my busy life, I still needed my breaks away from being a mother, boss lady and wife. I was way overdue for one. Chris was coming back home on Friday from being gone for the past two months, so I was determined to get a break before then. My girls knew I had a sitter, so they planned for us to go out, and that's what we did.

It was me, Michelle, Chanel, Gracie, Allie and Gina. We went out to dinner and bowling afterwards. We had lots of fun. We had this group of guys next to our lane. It was four of them. They all were flirtatious and fine. My girls flirted back, of course. Gracie pushed them away and I was a married woman, so it was a no-go for me too, but of course, they didn't give up. I tried ignoring them, as I bowled, drank and tripped with my girls.

Next thing I know, one of the guys came walking up to me. He was fine as fuck. Ok, I will admit that. He was maybe 5'11, beautiful, healthy red skin, looked Dominican or mixed. He had a cute hair-cut, his facial hair was neat, his teeth were white and straight; he had grey eyes, and was tatted all over, slim-toned, and he even had swag. They all were cute, actually. He came over and introduced himself to me as Anthony. He shook my hand and asked me what my name was. I started to lie, but with all my drunk-ass girls, I'm sure by the end of the night one would have ended up calling me Tara, so I just kept it real.

"I'm Tara," I told him.

He looked me directly in my eyes and said, "Wow, beautiful name for a beautiful woman."

As he looked me in my eyes, I gazed back into his. His skin complexion, with his eye color, did something to me... I couldn't explain. I can honestly say, Chris was not on my mind at all, as I spoke to Anthony. Especially, since we were going through our shit lately.

"Where are you from? If you don't mind me asking," Anthony said.

"Here," I told him.

"So am I! How old are you?"

I told him, "27"

"How old are you?" I asked.

He said he was 29. We got into kids and I found out he didn't have any and that he wasn't dating either. He asked me if I was dating and my mind went blank. As bad as I wanted to tell him no, I just kept it real and told him I had recently gotten married.

"So, I'm assuming I can't get your number," he asked.

Chris and I didn't go through each other's phones, but we never talked about us having friends either. I didn't know what to tell him. He was fine as hell, man.

At times when Chris was in Atlanta, I did get lonely. I would love to have someone to talk to. I was in between a rock and a hard place. If I turned him down, I probably would never see him again. I was confused. I was drunk, and my mind wasn't working as fast as it normally did. I was indecisive. As bad as I wanted to give him my number and more, I couldn't. I turned him down. I told him I was married and that was that.

I always seemed to attract the cutest men, at the wrong times. When he left from by me, I started thinking. *What type of man really tries to get a girl's number after being told she is married? Did he not care because all he wanted was pussy anyways, or was it a test to see how loyal I am?*

Chanel came over to me and was like, "Girl, I see how you was chatting it up with little Dominican over here. I see you, married woman!"

Chanel missed nothing, ok? Nothing at all... ever! We all went to the bar to grab more drinks and we were talking about the dudes. So, apparently, they all were brothers. They came to the bowling alley almost every Saturday.

Now that I knew that, if I wanted Anthony later on, I knew where to find him. A bitch had plans, ok? I wasn't doubting Chris and I, but shit, you never knew what would happen. Especially, when things started getting rocky only six months into our marriage.

Weeks went by and things started to get worse at home. Seemed like the more time that went by, the more frustrating it was for me to deal with Chris' bullshit. He was still gone the majority of the time. I was wondering what the purpose of being married was, when I often felt alone. Things were so much better before we got married. As much as I hated to regret our marriage, I found myself doing so more often than I'd like.

Since he was never home with us, I decided that baby girl and I was going to him. Atlanta, here we come! It wasn't a surprise. Unfortunately, he knew we were coming. After gathering our shit, we headed to the airport to catch our flight. After an hour of being at the airport, I got a call.

It was from the boutique. One of my employees called and told me that Michelle didn't show up. I was furious! Pissed the fuck off. I felt like I had another kid, when it came to her. When it came to showing up to work, and on time, she was horrible at it! She was too hungover to call or show, or maybe she was sick, and sometimes, she just didn't feel like it. Every excuse in the book, I've heard from her. I was over all the bullshit that came with her.

I couldn't call Chanel; she had the day off. She took her mom to brunch. She had a change of heart after running into her at Walmart and saw that she was clean now. After I lost Mom, she constantly talked about finding her mom. Realizing how short life is, she wanted to better their relationship while the opportunity was still there. I couldn't call her in and ruin that for them. So, that left only one person to go in and that was me.

I had no choice but to cancel my flight and waste money; all to figure out what was going on with Michelle. I called and called her but got no answer. I went by her house, but Allie said she wasn't there. She told me she went out last night and hadn't seen her. I didn't know if I should be worried or pissed. I was a little in between the both. In the past, I'd let too much shit slide and I was done being nice.

Since nobody had seen her or knew where she was, I went back to the boutique. All I could think of was that maybe she was drunk somewhere or laid up under some random-ass dude, again, that she met at the club. I really felt like the oldest. She needed to get her life together. After three hours of me being at the boutique, I got a phone call from an unknown number. It was Michelle.

When I answered the phone, I said hello and then an automated voice came on, asking me if I would accept the charges that applied to the collect call. I said yes, and then Michelle came on. She told me she was in jail because she went out last night and something happened, but she couldn't explain at that time. She needed me to bail her out. I told her I was on the way. I went to get the bitch out of jail, although I wanted to leave her there.

Ignorant to how that bondsman shit works, I tried calling people who had done it before in the past. I called Chanel, but she didn't pick up. I tried calling Chris and he didn't pick up either. Damn! Seemed like nobody knew how to answer their damn phone when I was the one calling. With no help from anyone else, I had no choice but to figure it out on my own.

I Googled some bail bondsman and just dived right in. She got out maybe an hour later. When she got in the car, I immediately went in on her.

"Well, what the fuck happened?"

"Chill, ok," Michelle said.

"I can't fuckin' chill, Michelle, I can't! Do you wanna know why I can't chill? Huh? I had to cancel my trip to the A and waste money on tickets I can't use and rearrange my life because of your bullshit! So, what's up," I said, in a furious voice.

"Ok, damn! Feels like I'm sitting in the car with Mom right now!"

"And it feels like you're my second child, so what?"

"Ok, so I went out with one of my male friends last night and he sells weed or whatever. He had initially drove us there in his car but was too drunk to drive home. Not knowing he had drugs in the car, I offered to drive, since I didn't have much to drink. Apparently, he had a taillight out, so the cops pulled us over. He asked for license and registration, I gave it to him. Everything was cool.

The cop was taking a long time and asked a lot of questions, so my friend got annoyed. He started to get loud and he was cursing at the cop. I was trying to calm him, and the cop asked him numerous times to calm down, but he refused. The officer asked him to step out the car and he did, but he started acting crazy, so he locked both of us up. I found out there was no insurance on the vehicle and drugs was in the car. He didn't claim the drugs, so I was charged with it. It's so fucked up, Tara," Michelle explained.

"Well, Michelle, I'm sorry you had to go through that, but I've told you many times to leave those sorry-ass niggas alone, to cut back on the partying and stop drinking. You don't listen! I guess since I'm the younger one, you figure I don't know what the hell I'm talking about. Well, guess what; I do! You are my sister and I love you! We are all we got, but I can't continue to do this with you! I can't continue to go back and forth with you and enable you to make sure you do what you are supposed to do. I have more than enough on my own plate to worry about. I can't continue to accept what you do in regards to your job either! The no call no shows, the showing up hungover and fixing the mistakes you continually make on a daily basis because you are not focused... It's not fair to me and it's bad for my business. I will always be your sister, but I refuse to be your mom, babysitter or boss. I am going to have to replace you," I told her.

She sat in the car and just looked at me, before flipping out.

"Replace me? How the fuck are you gonna fire your own sister? I've been bustin' my ass in your shop since day one! I've been there for you every step of the way. I've tried everything I could to help you in every way because I knew you've been going through a lot. The one time you aren't able to go and be up under Chris, or can't go on vacation and have fun, you want to fire me? That's the shit you have to deal with as a boss! You wanna be a "boss" so bad, right? Well, deal with it! How am I supposed to pay my bills? How? Do you know how long it will take me to find another job? I guess you wouldn't! You get money and forget where you came from! It's ok, Tara, fuck you and your shop," Michelle said to me, as she got out my car and slammed the door.

I wanted to get out and beat her ass so fuckin' bad, but I sat in my car and gathered myself before pulling off. I couldn't believe that bitch! I helped her almost every time she called me. I've been dealing with her bitchy attitude all my life; and although I hated the type of person she was, and how she acted, I put it all aside to better our relationship and come closer with her. I understood how she felt, and I would appreciate it if she understood how I felt - for once; but as selfish as Michelle is, she never will.

When I got home I feed and washed Armani and put her to bed. Getting myself prepared to unwind from the day I had, I took my shower, fixed some red wine and hopped in bed. When I picked up the phone to call Chris, he was calling me.

"Hey, baby!"

"Hey!" I responded. He could hear in my voice that something was wrong. He wanted to know what was going on and he wanted to know immediately. Never having a chance to let him know we weren't going to make it to him, again, he asked about that too.

I told him how my day went and about the big argument Michelle and I had, which explained why we weren't in Atlanta. That wasn't the only thing I wanted to talk to him about. Discussing how I'd been feeling lately was a priority. There were some changes that needed to be made to better our household and make my life a little smoother.

When I started explaining that, he started flipping out. He was cursing at me, getting loud and argumentative . He felt like I was saying that he was a bad dad and husband. It was a big mess and I had already dealt with enough that day, so I hung up.

I had never seen that side of Chris before. He had never cursed at me, in all the time I've known and been with him. He was a very private person, so for him to get loud in his club and while people were around, was unusual for him. That was by far the biggest fight we'd ever had, in fact... the only! I didn't know if he was overwhelmed with working and being a new dad or if he was drunk.

I knew he drunk a lot back in the day, before I met him, but he said he didn't care to drink anymore. He went to rehab and put that part of his life behind him. When he drunk around me, he would only have a glass of wine. I was tempted to call him back, but I didn't want things to get worse. He didn't bother calling me back, so I said fuck it. As I sat in the bed thinking about everything, I started to wonder. Well, why didn't he call much earlier when he realized we didn't show at the time I told him we were landing? It made me wonder if he even cared.

I'm a softy for certain people, and Chris is one of those people; so, guess what? I ended up calling him back maybe an hour later. From the sound of his background, he was at the club. While he talked to me, I listened really hard. I had never heard or seen how he acted when he was drunk, because like I said, he never really drunk around me. I wasn't sure if he was drunk, but I definitely could tell he had a few drinks.

As the night went on, more and more thoughts ran through my head. I wondered if he was at his own club, working or out partying. I was concerned that he didn't mention to me that he was drinking again.

Trying to take my mind off Chris, I started thinking about Michelle and I's argument. I needed to figure out where I went wrong. I tried contacting her but got no answer. Every time I would go by her apartment, one of the girls would say she wasn't home. I started to worry! I knew she was upset but didn't know she would have taken it that far.

I felt bad about firing her, but my mind was made up and I wasn't turning back. I had to remind myself she was a grown-ass woman who had the same opportunities I did. She chose to live the life she was living. She needed to learn how to stand on her own two feet, and learn from her mistakes, like I did.

When Chanel returned to work the next day, she bragged about her brunch date with her mom. Things went well for them. Ms. Sherlene was clean now. She had left Mr. Harold alone completely, she apologized to her for everything, and was looking good again. Ms. Sherlene didn't have a stable home, so Chanel was considering moving out of the apartment her and

Norris shared. She wanted to get a new place for her and her mom.

Everybody's life was starting to come together except mine. Everyone seemed happy around me and pleased with how they were living. Meanwhile, I was stuck wondering what the hell my husband was really up to when he told me he needed to go to Atlanta for work. I didn't want to be that insecure bitch, but I wasn't going to be naive either. He was coming home, so with a date night planned, we were finally going to talk things through.

If it was nothing, I really needed him to tell me that. I needed to know that he was still loyal to me and was loving only me. I needed to know that his family mattered most to him and that he would make changes to ensure his wife was happy, and be involved in his daughter's life as much as possible. I needed to know if he was in his club working that night, or if he was drinking again. I needed to know if he went to Atlanta to get away from us. I needed answers, I deserved them.

Chapter 11

"A Buried Demon"

When Chris arrived home, I was still at the boutique, getting paperwork done and training the new employee I promoted, since I fired Michelle. I gave him the time of our reservation and told him I would be home within the next few hours to get ready. I was turning things around and decided to show him a good time , like how he'd done for me in the past.

When I got home, he wasn't there. I called his phone and he didn't answer. I started calling around, but no one seemed to have heard from him, (well, so they said). It was clear he'd already been home because he had the place a mess, his bags were thrown all over the place.

I left Armani with the sitter and sat in the house, drinking wine and watching movies, until Chris decided to make his way home. After about two hours of waiting, I started to get pissed. I was completely worried at first, but as time went on, I got angrier. I couldn't believe this motherfucker had really stood me up. I was busy all day, but instead of feeling guilty, I made time for my husband. I rearranged my day for him. I changed my plans, all for him; and guess what, the time and effort I'd put in to please and make him happy was all for nothing. It was obvious he was caught up or busy with something or someone else that was more important than I was.

At 2am, I started nodding off. I had a long day, and since my plans were cancelled, I wanted to get some rest; but I refused to go to sleep until this motherfucker showed up… Not to make sure he was safe, well… that too, but to get to the bottom of what the hell was going on with him and why the sudden changes. Chris had never done this to me.

Now that he stood me up, ignored my calls and didn't return them, it was a big deal. I didn't know how to handle it. My expectations were high, when it came to him, because he never half stepped. Tolerating this was a no-go for me. I know I dealt with a lot of shit, when it came to Norris, but I was young then. I'm a grown-ass woman now, and it was just some things I wasn't going to stand for anymore. This, being one of them.

I was sitting on the bed, sipping my wine, trying my best to stay awake. About 3:15am, I heard keys turning in the door. As he walked in, he made a hell of a lot of noise. It sounded like he was stumbling and grabbing on the wall. I heard glass breaking from him leaning on my décor and knocking things over, so I hopped up out the bed. When I got up, I stood in the doorway of my room in disbelief and disgust. Sure enough, he was out drinking.

Never did I ever want to be an insecure bitch, but when I saw that he was drinking, I couldn't help but to think the worse. I called all the guys he could have possibly been with, and they all told me they didn't see him. Now, I had it in my mind he was with a bitch. I wanted to give Chris the benefit of the doubt, but I did that with Norris and he played my ass. I was getting to the bottom of it before the night was over.

Not only did he come in the house at 3:15am, without calling or answering my calls, but he stood me up for our date and went out to go get drunk with God knows who. I was so thankful I had left Armani with a sitter, because this was going to be one hell of a night.

Chris' night may have been coming to an end but guess what... Mine was just getting started! I flipped the fuck out, ok! I was already pissed about the shit I'd been dealing with lately. Everybody had been getting on my last nerve. Everybody had been doing me dirty and making me feel like I wasn't good enough. When Chris came in, it triggered all my anger.

He was one of the few people I leaned on to help me deal with the shit I went through. In fact, he was the only person, when I had issues with my girls. And now, here he was causing me more pain than any of them did. Not giving a fuck about how much he upset and disappointed me.

I stood in the doorway and looked at Chris for about ten minutes, as he walked around, stumbling and drooling, barely able to hold his head up and talking to himself as he fell on the floor. I walked over to him and stood over him, as he laid on the floor overly intoxicated, and stared at him some more.

Finally, I spoke.

"So, I see you're back drinking? Where the hell were you tonight? Do you think it's acceptable, as a married man, to be out all night without calling? Ignoring my text and calls? Coming in at 3:15am and not telling me where you were? This shit isn't ok, Chris! Not to mention, you stood me up to be with someone that was obviously more important than I am! Were they more important than me, Chris," I asked him, rigidly.

Looking up at me, he laid on the floor, staring.

There was a moment of silence. He got up slowly, brushed up against me and pushed me in the corner with my back against the wall. Breathing heavily, with one hand around my throat and the other pointing in my face, he said, "Listen, bitch! Don't you ever...ever question anything I do again! I am a grown-ass man, you hear me? I don't have to answer to anyone, not even my *'wife!'* If you don't like the shit I'm telling you, then leave me!"

He held me for 30 seconds more, before he decided to let me go. He looked like a monster. There was this look in his eyes I had never seen before. I stood there, holding my neck. It was hard for me to swallow, even a little difficult for me to breath, because of how tight he gripped it. Tears filled my eyes and as he spoke, they continued to roll down my cheeks. He eventually walked off and I stood there in agony.

I couldn't believe he'd really put his hands on me. I didn't know who he was anymore, or what that demon inside of him was capable of. Chris had never laid hands on me before. He had never spoken to me in that way either. I started to question who he really was.

"Maybe we should take a break and be apart for a while! You turned out to be a person I never thought you'd be! You don't love me, Chris....you don't love me," I cried out to him.

I dropped to the floor with my back against the wall and my hands on my head, face buried into my knees. Next thing I knew, he grabbed my hair and said, "We should do what, bitch? Answer me, you fuckin' slut!"

Where was all this coming from? I thought to myself. He slapped me so hard on the left side of my face I felt it stinging for hours after. I knew for sure it was going to leave a mark, but that didn't stop me.

As he held my hair tightly, I got up. He pushed me back down, but he was too drunk and weak to overpower me that time. Somehow, I got up and got loose. When I did, I kneed him in the nuts and cocked my arm as far back as I could and boxed him in the center of his face.

He hollered, jumped around and stumbled, as the pain hit him. I was proud for standing up for myself. There was no way I would be able to beat a man, but I wasn't going out without trying. When he leaned over the chair, I kicked him in the back, causing the sofa to slide across the hardwood floor from underneath him. I didn't know what had gotten into me. I guess I was really at my breaking point.

I went in the room, grabbed one of my bags and started shoving clothes in it. As I ran around the house, grabbing my clothes and necessities, I hollered at him,

"Is this how you want a guy to treat your daughter," I asked, but he didn't respond.

I didn't hear a sound or any movement. Concerned, I ran back in the living room, where he sat on the floor, to make sure he was ok. Once I realized he was fine, I continued.

"You are a sorry piece of shit, you know that?"

He looked up at me, looked deeply in my eyes and said, "Fuck you! You know what you are? A no-good, slutty-ass wife! You keep secrets and expect a good man like me to be loyal to you, after all the shit you've done?"

I wanted to slap the shit out of him, but I knew it would only add fuel to the fire and make things worse. I just stood there for a second, and then I walked off. I went back to the room to grab my bag and walked around the living room, looking for my purse. When I found it, I grabbed it and I started to head out. I unlocked the door, started to swing it open and walk out, but then Chris stopped me. I was so close to getting the hell out and away from his ass.

He pushed the door closed so hard the pictures on the wall moved. He snatched my purse from me and threw it across the room. He tugged on my bag, but I refused to let it go.

Then, he grabbed my hair, again, this time wrapping it around his hand multiple times. He jerked my neck back and said, "Where the fuck do you think you are going? To be with Norris? To be with your potential baby's father? Are you about to run to him and tell him that I hurt you? Or are you going to fuck and suck his dick, again?"

That explained why Chris was changing and why he was so angry lately. I was stunned. I stood in front of him, speechless, thinking about who could have told him this.

"Yeah, I know! I know that you fucked him! I know that he was over here the night you got back home from me! I know you invited him to the baby shower because he could potentially be Armani's father! Yeah, bitch, I know everything," he continued.

"And you fucking lied to me! In my face! Multiple times," Chris said, louder.

"I was happy to be a dad! I was ready to give her the world! Even give you the world! I married you because I thought you was the one, Tara! Instead, you lied to me! You gave my pussy away! You are taking the best thing that ever happened to me away. You and that beautiful baby girl I watched grow and come out of you was all I ever wanted. I catered to you and made sure that both of you were good, since day one. I can't believe this shit!"

Chris continued, "You ain't nothin' but a fuckin' whore. You ain't no better than the other bitches I dealt with."

Not only had I never seen this man so angry and upset, but I had never seen him so hurt either. He had done so many things to me that night and hurt me both physically and mentally, but I stood by him. I comforted him because I knew how he felt. I know I should have walked away, since he put his hands on me, but love is dangerous. It will have you puttin' up with shit you know you're too good for, and that's where I was at the moment.

I was guilty for not being honest with him from the beginning. It was fucked up he had to find out the way he did. All I could say to him was, "I'm sorry." I really wanted to tell him, but I didn't know how to. A night like this was what I feared.

I felt like he was me, and I was Norris. The man I loved unconditionally was being hurt by the one he put all his trust and love into. I bashed Norris for treating me horribly, breaking my heart and humiliating me, but in reality, I was no better than him.

My mind was racing. I had so much going on. I had so much to think about. What really bothered me most was who the hell told him all of this. There were only a few people at the table when I spoke about it. All the people there were women I thought I could trust. I didn't know how the information got back to Chris, but I was definitely going to find out.

I didn't know who to trust. Was it Michelle, because we fell out? Did Gracie tell Josh and Josh told Chris, because of course that's his brother? Or was it Chanel? She wouldn't have a purpose behind it, though. It wasn't like we was beefin'. She'd never crossed me in a way like that. Then again, it seemed like she was attracted to him from the beginning, with the slick comments she made from time to time.

Then, I thought about Norris... Was he the one that told all of this because he wanted to ruin things with us to get me back? Was Chris out with Norris that night? Oh my, I couldn't believe it. Well... I could. Maybe it was him! I didn't know for sure, though. I didn't want to approach him about it, if it wasn't him. I didn't want to give him any ideas he hadn't already thought about.

Whoever it was, really crossed the line. They really had it out for us. They really wanted to tear my family apart. *That ain't nothin' but the devil*, I thought to myself, shaking my head. I realized right then and there that our enemies were actually the ones closest to us.

I needed to know where that information came from. I had to know! I was definitely getting to be bottom of it. They were not getting away with it. I just couldn't believe that I was so loyal to my girls and one of them went behind my back and betrayed me.

For the next couple of days, baby girl and I stayed in a nice suite where nobody knew where we were. I ignored calls, unless it was from the shop. Thankfully, nobody needed to call me, and things were running smoothly. I needed a break. I needed time to really think about what happened the other night and process all the information I received. I was focusing on the next move I was going to make.

Having my daughter around Chris wasn't an option. Seeing how he acted when he got drunk intimidated me. Not knowing what he would do to me, the next time he got drunk, or what he would do to my daughter, knowing that she could potentially be someone else's kid scared the shit out of me. Chris was a demon on the liquor.

My life had taken such a big turn. Who would have ever known I would be so unhappy? I was married with a beautiful kid. I owned a big, beautiful home at 27. I was finally living my dream as a boutique owner, had tons of money and I had an awesome husband, so I thought, and my girls was here whenever I needed them.

As I sat down, I realized materialistic shit didn't matter to me. I was happier when I didn't have all of this. I was happier when I didn't have so much responsibility and pressure on myself. I wanted to give up everything, realizing that money couldn't buy happiness. Quitting wasn't an option either. I couldn't turn back.

Chapter 12

"Private Investigating"

I had a lot of time to think and I came up with a plan. That plan required me to ignore my feelings, set aside my anger and pain and focus on the bigger picture. I had to figure out who was really loyal to me, my situations and my secrets. My husband was on the line, my happiness, my family and my future. I had to be selfish and think about me and mine, this time.

A week had passed. I hadn't seen or spoken to Chris since it all went down. So, I called him up and had him meet me at a restaurant... A public place, so things wouldn't get out of hand. I hoped that he actually showed up this time. Surprisingly, he did.

When he came, he looked different, as if he fell off a little bit. The Chris I knew always made sure he dressed nice, his hair was right, he smelled and looked good, but the Chris that met with me really showed that he was going through some shit and didn't give a fuck about how anybody felt about him or what people thought of him. It was a little depressing.

He ordered himself some tequila. I knew the meeting wouldn't be good. It was 2 o' clock in the afternoon and he was already drinking. I started thinking, maybe his problem was more out of hand than I thought. He never spoke, so as I sat across from him, watching him down shots of tequila. I started the conversation off with a sincere apology.

"I'm sorry, Chris! None of this was supposed to happen like this! My intentions never were to hurt you!"

He still didn't speak, so I continued.

"I love you and I have never seen you like this. Your anger and drinking has gotten out of control and I'm worried about you! Talk to me, tell me what's going on with you!"

He looked at me, leaned into me and grabbed my face with one hand, as he whispered to me,

"You are the cause of all of this! You caused me to turn back to drinking! You've been lying to me! You've been fucking your ex and you don't fuckin' respect me! You did me wrong, Tara! I fuckin' loved you!"

He squeezed my cheeks harder, as he spoke, leaving them sore, once he decided to let me go.

"You said you loved me. What does that mean, Chris?"

He didn't say anything.

"So, after one fight, you're giving up on us? Did I ever mean anything to you besides a piece of pussy to fuck?"

Chris stood up from the table, pushing the table on me, hollering, "Bitch, I married you. How could you say that bullshit?"

After leaving a fifty on the table to cover the alcohol he drunk, along with the tip, he ran out the restaurant and I ran behind him. Everyone was turning to look at us. People started whispering and pointing. He embarrassed me badly.

"Chris, wait," I hollered.

"Fuck you, Tara! Fuck you!"

I grabbed Chris' shirt and asked, "Why are you treating me like this?"

"I guess you really are a stupid bitch! Did everything I say in there go in one ear and out the other?"

"You know what, Chris, I'ma give you your time!"

Right before going our separate ways, I told him it's best we take some time apart and that we stayed in separate places.

He responded with, "I agree. You keep the house, here's the keys. My things are practically gone and I'll see you when I see you."

After dropping the keys in my hand, he walked off to his car. I felt like I was being dropped. I was confused. He was in a rage, just the other night, and refused for me to walk out on him, but here he was doing to me what he didn't want me to do to him. All I could ask myself was, "What the fuck just happened?" I didn't plan for it to go like this. I didn't even know if I wanted to go back to the house.

I knew for sure he was seeing another chick. What nigga walks out on his wife like that over a petty fight? Or was it? I still didn't know if I was the wrong one in this situation. Well, I was, but we were equally wrong. He still hadn't owned up to his shit, nor did he apologize. I really felt like him not showing up to the damn dinner was why we were in this predicament in the first place. I was convinced that our troubles were him and his informants' fault.

I was still standing in the parking lot with a dropped jaw and keys in my hand, thinking about all of this. Chris had already pulled off and went on about his business. I still couldn't believe what the fuck he had said to me and what the fuck had happened.

As I broke down in the middle of the parking lot, I prayed. I hadn't spoken to God like I should, but I prayed. I asked for guidance, I begged for strength, and asked Him to watch over and heal me from the pain I was feeling. I asked Him to reveal to me the truth about everything. I asked Him to show me who my true friends were and remove the ones that meant me no good.

I opened my eyes, closed my hands and held my keys. I walked to my car and went on with my day. The first person I reached out to was Gracie. I asked her if we could meet. Luckily, she was free. She said they were running some errands, so I invited both her and Josh to lunch. Maybe Josh knew who told Chris what he knew. She agreed to meet with me and told me she had something she wanted to talk to me about anyways.

I was anxious to know what she had to say. It was killing me to know what she wanted to talk about. Hoping she would tell me everything I needed to know and ending my search for answers.

I arrived about thirty minutes early. I was in the area and had nothing else to do.

I waited for about twenty minutes before they walked in. When I saw them pull up, I got butterflies in my stomach. I didn't know what to expect and she had Josh with her. If she said the wrong thing around him, it could make things worse. I tried to calm myself and prepare for the worse, but it was hard.

When they came to the table, Josh hugged me.

"Long time no see," he said to me.

"I know. I've just been so caught up with work and that little girl; I stay busy," I replied.

Little did he know, it was way beyond that and his fucking brother was the real problem. I just left it at that, though. When I saw Gracie, she was glowing. She always took care of herself, but she looked better than ever.

"Hey, girl, I missed you," she said to me, as she hugged me.

I held her tightly and started to get teary-eyed. I really did miss my friend, but if I cried, it would say so much more than I came to talk about. It was a struggle trying to hold back my tears, but I did.

"I missed you more! You are glowing, boo, lookin' better than ever," I told her.

She looked at Josh and smiled, as he smiled back. I looked at them both, thinking to myself, *what the hell was really going on?*

"Well, thank you," she replied, blushing.

I could tell they were happy together. The happiness that showed on her face was what I thought would never stop showing on mine, after getting with Chris, but I was wrong.

"So, what you been up to? I haven't heard from you in a while. I was just asking Josh if he spoke to you or Chris."

"Girl, Chris and I have been so busy with work and our little diva, we hardly have time for ourselves anymore. Life is taking a toll on us these days," I replied, fake smiling and laughing the best way I knew how.

"How is my niece? I haven't seen her in a while. I'm upset with you about that, by the way," Josh said.

"She is good, she's so smart, getting big so fast. She is a handful," I explained, and then showed them pictures of her that I had in my phone.

"I want to get her one day," Josh said to me.

"Sure! I could always use a break," I replied, laughing.

"Well, we need the practice, because in just a little bit we will have our own," Gracie chimed in.

"What? Oh my goodness, I didn't know. Congratulations!" They both thanked me at the same time. I jumped out of my seat to hug Gracie.

"So, is that what you wanted to talk to me about," I asked.

"Well, that's just half of it," Gracie said.

"You know I'm modeling and was going to take a break from work due to my belly, but I still need income. I was wondering if you had room at your boutique for me," Gracie said.

"Of course! I could always use more help. I'll go down there today and see where you can fit in," I told her.

"So, Josh, when was the last time you spoke to your brother?" I asked him.

"I really couldn't tell you, Tara; maybe two weeks ago. It's been a while. We hardly ever go that long without talking. We normally talk twice a week - at least. I tried calling him, but shit, he doesn't answer. I don't know what I've done to him," Josh said.

"Yeah, I know, y'all normally talk often. I wouldn't take it personal, though. With the back and forth, he is constantly on the go. You know how much he loves that club," I told Josh, as I sipped my wine.

"Yeah, you're right."

"Well, it was good seeing y'all. I need to get going. Gracie, I'll text you about the job once I figure it all out; and Josh, I'll be sure to text you about getting Armani," I said, as I winked at them.

They both stood up and hugged me. I walked out of the restaurant and went to my car.

I couldn't believe they were expecting, but I was happy for them. As I sat there and spoke to them both, I felt their attitudes and feelings were genuine. I really couldn't convince myself that they had anything to do with all the drama. Because of that, I wanted to talk to Gracie about what was really going on later. I needed her help. She may have been the only one I had left.

Before heading home, I headed to the shop, and on the way there, I tried calling Michelle. I called multiple times, but she still didn't answer. She was taking me firing her to the extreme. So much time had passed, and she was still ignoring me. I started to believe that it was way beyond that. I just hoped she wasn't assuming that I was calling for the money she owed me for bailing her out because I wasn't. I had money, and if she didn't have it to give back, it was fine. I just knew it wasn't about me firing her, though.

I swung by the shop to see how things were going, and see where we could use the extra help, so Gracie could hop in. When I went by, everything looked good. Chanel was there, and I spoke to her, but I kept it short. I brought her in the office and spoke to her about business. I took that time to ask her how things had been holding up there. She started giving me a rundown and after, she asked what I've been up to because she missed me.

I didn't say too much. I just told her I had a lot going on and that I needed to take care of things. She kind of brushed off what I said and said ok. Then, she said, "You know what, Gracie can cover me for a few days, actually. I need to go out of town. You've been MIA lately, you haven't even heard what's been going on!" Ok, so, Chanel never goes out of town. She barely does anything or cares to do anything, but I just sat there and listened.

"So, where are you going, missy," I asked, in the most fakest voice.

"So, let me tell you what's been going on. Long story short, I was on social media a couple weeks back and I saw that Andrew, your man's business partner, sent me a friend request, right? A day after I accepted it, he DM's me. We ended up exchanging numbers and have been talking ever since. He wants to fly me out to Atlanta and spend some time with him. If I can get time off, or whenever I get time off, I'm going! All expenses on him and I need this getaway, bitch," Chanel explained.

"Say what? That's good! So, do you like him," I asked her.

"Hell yeah! He's fine, he is cool as fuck, he has money and more money," she said back.

"I'll make something happen, so you can go out and be with your boo. How about you train Gracie this week with as much as you can, and I'll help her this weekend, that way you can leave this weekend," I told her.

Speaking about Atlanta with Chanel, I started to wonder where and who Chris was with. I hadn't heard from him in a while. Truth was, I really missed him. I called him, but the phone just rang. I called twice, and it did the same thing. The second time, I left a voicemail. I also sent three text messages, but he never responded. I guess he was living his best life. No kid and no wife to worry about. He hadn't checked on us. I wanted to rebuild our relationship, better our marriage, and do what it took to make things right again. Instead, the little things he did pushed me away. It made me wonder if I should stop giving a fuck.

The next day, I called Gracie and filled her in on what she would be doing at the shop. Covering Chanel's shift and making sure my money was right was easy. I normally handled it, for the most part, but with everything going on in my life, I could use a few extra hands and eyes. Thankfully, she agreed to it.

While I had her on the phone, I vented, and I let everything out. We were on the phone for almost three and a half hours. We started out laughing and ended with crying. I needed to talk to someone; someone that I could trust. I trusted her. I knew it wasn't her. I felt it in my heart and I trusted in God.

Chapter 13

"Reclaiming What's Mine"

So, when Chanel came back from Atlanta, she called me. Thankfully, she caught me at a good time. I was home relaxing, so I had time to talk and listen. She had so much to talk to me about. She told me how she enjoyed herself and how she spent lots of time with Andrew, with Chris around too. I was happy to see that she was happy. It took her a while to finally date again, after she got raped.

She went on to tell me about my husband. Chanel told me how he was drunk in the club and all over other women. I was still on the fence about Chanel. I didn't know if I should trust her or not.

It seemed like one thing after another. That was valuable information, though. Chris was trippin'. He wasn't calling or caring about me, so him being over other women was believable for sure. I didn't expect my husband to run out and mess around after one, simple argument. It was also quite interesting to know that those actions went on in his club. Seemed to me like professionalism didn't matter to him anymore. Instead, he was out being the whore he called me.

I knew he was drinking more than ever before, but at his place of business? This definitely wasn't like Chris. "He was in Atlanta to take care of business," as he always told me. Ha! Now,

I started to wonder if 'taking care of business' meant other women and liquor bottles.

I had tons of questions I wanted to ask her. I needed to know more details, but I couldn't ask. Chanel didn't know I was having trouble in my marriage, and being that she was still suspect, I wanted to keep it that way.

Should I call Chris and ask him about what Chanel told me? Should I just ignore it and let him be? I didn't know what to do. I still wanted to work things out with him. Marriage counseling was heavy on my mind, lately, but hearing what Chanel had to say about him made me wonder if I should lose hope in us. How he'd been acting lately, I wasn't convinced that this was what he still wanted. Hell, I wasn't sure if I truly wanted to stay either, after having flashbacks and nightmares of the terrifying night we had.

I sat on the bed and dropped tears. I was angry. I was confused. I was skeptical. I was discouraged... I was at my breaking point and ready to give up on us!

I called Chris, and guess what? He finally answered, after weeks and weeks of ignoring me. When he picked up, he didn't say anything.

"Hello," I said.

"Yeah," he responded.

"Good to hear from you. I'm happy you answered. I tried calling you for weeks."

"I know! I wasn't ready to talk."

"Oh, ok! Well, I miss you, and I love you!"

"I miss you and love you too."

"The last time we sat down, it didn't turn out how I thought it would, but I wanted to know if you were available to sit down with me again."

"Yeah, we can."

"Are you in town?"

"In the A."

"Ok, well, how about I come out there tomorrow and we can figure some things out?"

"Ok, cool," he said, and then we both hung up.

I was excited and ready to see him. I was determined to make the best of this trip. I wanted the old Chris back! You know, the guy that went out of his way to make me happy? The guy who showed me love and affection on the daily. The guy who made sure to pick up on the first ring when I called and got upset with himself if he missed my phone call. The guy who stopped whatever it was he was doing to be there for me. The guy that took me out and showed me off. The guy who I was proud to call my husband.

When I got to Atlanta, I caught an Uber and went to the house. Chris wasn't there. So, I used that time to my advantage. I looked around for any evidence or clues that showed he was having an affair. Call me a crazy bitch if you want, but we all know any woman who feels her man is cheating, definitely snoops in his shit. So, I'm walking around, I'm looking in and around shit, I'm sniffing clothes and covers, but I didn't find anything. I was half-way through the house, at that point. He had to be really good at hiding shit. I knew he had someone in that house.

If he was treating me like shit, he was drunk all the time, he worked in a club where lots of women came, he was all over women in front of my best friend and was living hundreds of miles away in a big-ass house, there was no way he'd been alone all that time. There was no damn way!

I'm much wiser than that to even believe such a thing. So, I continued to peep around, but I got thirsty and went to get something to drink out the fridge. I'm lookin' in the fridge and find chocolate syrup. Chris hated chocolate syrup. He couldn't stand the taste of it one bit. So, who the fuck was in there? Whose chocolate syrup was that and how was it used? I was ready to call that nigga and cut up.

I had to really keep my cool and remember I couldn't be trippin' right now. I didn't want to ruin it, although, I felt like my questions should be answered. I was going to get back on his good side, get my husband back, and then hit him with all the questions I had. Sure enough, I drained the remaining chocolate syrup out and trashed the bottle. No more of whatever went on was going on up in here.

I went to the club where Chris was. Most of the girls who worked there knew me, but I wasn't there in a while, so I decided to show my face and claim my territory. Yes, I walked up in that bitch like everything was dandelions and roses between my husband and me. They seemed shocked to see me, as if they heard about us though.

I played it off, kept it cute and kept it movin'. I walked around, just observing, and then I went to the bar and grabbed me a drink. One girl who worked there loved me. She would always talk to me, on the low, when I came and filled me in on what was going on, but she wasn't there. I asked one of the other bartenders where she was, and she said she'd gotten fired weeks prior. Not surprising! His sneaky-ass probably heard what she was up to.

After I got my drink, I sat at the bar for a little bit and the three girls went to the opposite side of the bar, huddling kind of. I didn't know if my mind was fucked up and playing tricks on me because I was having trust issues lately and was paranoid, or if those bitches was really on some funny shit.

So, I'm sippin' and lookin' at them with a "bitch, what, I'm ready" look on my face. I heard one girl whisper, "Who's that?" Since she wanted to be nosey and funny, I responded to her loudly, "Your boss' wife. Any issues?" and downed the rest of my drink, slammin' the glass on the counter. I was already in a bad mood and I dared a bitch to try me that day! She didn't say anything, she just frowned and got back to work. I hopped off the bar stool and walked off like a boss.

He probably was fuckin' that bitch that's why she gave me a funny look, but I didn't give a damn. I would really drive myself crazy tryin' to figure out what this man was doin' when I wasn't around. I never wanted my marriage to be like this. I had spoken to God many times already and asked Him to reveal to me what it was I needed to know. I trusted in Him... probably, the only man I trusted, actually, and left it in His hands. If that was one of his hoes, I would find out sooner than later. Oh, when I found out, it would be over for the both of them.

Probably about 10 minutes after dealing with Chris' nosey, disrespectful-ass employees, he came out and we left. That bitch was really asking for an ass whippin'. When we walked out the club, she whispered and giggled, while lookin' at us. I turned my head her way, stuck my tongue out and blew a kiss. I wasn't going to show out like how I really wanted to at that time, but I knew for sure I would see that bitch again.

We hopped in his car and left the club. We went back to the house and got ready for our night out. I was still pissed about the chocolate syrup I found, so I found a way to bring it up to see his reaction.

I actually went in the kitchen where he was and told him, "Hey, I used the last bit of chocolate syrup you had in the fridge for my ice cream. I thought you didn't like chocolate syrup anyways."

"That was Andrew's. It's cool. He left it the night all of us were here watching the game," he replied

Who is all of us, I wanted to ask, but I held that one in too. It was only a matter of time before I would be bringing all this shit back up.

He must have thought I had dumb bitch written on my forehead. That was probably the lamest lie he'd ever told me. He knew I knew better than that, but, again, I wasn't going to stress it. I wanted to keep the peace, for now, and deal with the bullshit later. I left him in the kitchen and went back to getting ready.

When we went out, we had a nice time. He took me to a fancy-ass Italian restaurant. It was fancy, but nothin' like that bougie one back in Charlotte he took me to. He wasn't drunk, and it felt like old times. By the grace of God, he finally apologized to me for everything he had done to me the night we fought. He spoke a lot that night and acknowledged a lot of things I came to discuss. He continued on to say that he still loves Mani and no matter what, he wanted to be a part of her life.

He hugged and kissed on me all night and told me how much he missed me and loved me. He even said he wanted to be back in the house and wanted to be a family again, like how we used to be. It was nice to hear him say the things I doubted him about. Then, I started thinkin', if he felt this way, why did Chanel tell me he was just hugged up with other women just a few days ago. Was he putting on a show or was Chanel tellin' lies?

After enjoyin' our night, we headed back to the house. I had a good time, but the night was getting better. We both went to take a shower. He hugged on me some more, kissed on my neck, fingered me and fucked me, just a little bit to get me and my pussy excited.

When we got out the shower, I sat on the edge of the bed and put some Bath & Body Works Thousand Wishes lotion all over my body. I pinned my hair up and put my bonnet on. I was getting ready for a good night. I hadn't had sex in months. That tease he gave me in the shower had me ready to get slammed.

I wanted it all. When I was just finishing up with the lotion, Chris walked in the room. I was completely naked. Since he teased me, I played the game along with him. When he walked in the room, I got on all fours at the edge of the bed, ass up, and crawled to the middle of the bed in the sexiest way I knew how. I could see him in the mirror behind me, getting harder and harder, as he walked up to me.

"Damn, girl, that ass look good!" he said.

I continued to tease him. I was already in the middle of the bed, lying down, by the time he got to me. I laid in the middle of the bed on my back, legs wide open and rubbed myself with one hand, and playing with my nipples with the other. He stood in front of the bed strokin' his shit, lookin' delicious as always. I was ready to stop teasin' and take it, but it was getting fun.

Like I said, I hadn't had sex in months, so while I teased Chris, I teased myself. He stood in front of me with his shit sticking straight out in front of him, ready to dive in me; and in less than two minutes, my juices were soaking the bed.

With my legs still wide, he crawled on the bed and started sucking on my clit. I thought I was going to cum as soon as he started. He did it for like three minutes, but I didn't want to cum yet, so I told him to get on top. He came up, kissing all over my body. Moving from my stomach to my breasts, to my neck, and then to my lips. I kissed this man like it was our first time. We kissed and kissed, and then all I felt was his fingers jamming into my pussy.

I moaned and moaned, as he rubbed on me, and shortly after, he penetrated me. When he did that, my body instantly dropped down on the bed, as if I was lifeless. I couldn't control it. That time when he put it in, he went deeper and deeper.

It took me back to the first time we ever sexed! It took me back to why I loved him! ...Back to why I married him and why I didn't want to be with anybody else! It took me back to why I didn't want him to be with anybody else! His shit had that type of power and control over me. He was the truth wit' it. He released all his anger in our sex. He started off slow and gentle, and then he sped up and got aggressive as hell. He knew I loved that shit! His sex was like a drug. I fiend for it and I could never get enough.

He flipped me over many times, as we switched positions several times. He had me get on top of the dresser and we laid on the floor. If he did fuck anybody else, there was no way their pussy was as good as mine because this nigga was buggin'. You could tell he really missed me and was overdue for some of my good shit. He may have his side bitches, but no bitch could lay it down like I do, and he knew that!

It was crazy, but things got even crazier! In all the time we fucked, we'd never tried anal. He never showed interest or asked about it, but that night he did. After we both came twice, he asked. We'd watched porn many times and I've seen it happen. It looked painful; and because of that, I was against it. Him askin' for it turned me off a little bit. I was finding every excuse not to do it. My biggest excuse, yet valid, was "Don't we need lube? We don't have any!"

I knew for sure it wasn't happening then. We didn't have lube, I never needed it. In my mind, I was like, *Damn I'm good*, but then this nigga pulled out a tube of lube. Pissed was an understatement. First of all, what the fuck was he doing with that? We never used it! Secondly, why was it used? What was really going on in this damn house? I didn't want to fuck anymore. There was a lot of things I wanted to address and brushed it off to keep the peace, but that one I couldn't let slide by me!

He told me he liked to use the lube to jerk off. I wasn't there, he didn't want to fuck anyone else, so he watched porn and jerked off. It was valid, and I respected it, but did I believe him? Not so much… He asked me, again, "Baby? Please, can we try it?

Just this one time, I promise." Focusing on pleasing my man so he didn't have to get it anywhere else, I agreed to do it.

As soon as we started it, I wanted to quit. Something so big going in such a tiny hole was beyond the pain I could handle. I wanted to cry. It felt like I was a virgin again, but worse. He went in, then more, and more. The pain I took, the discomfort I tolerated; all for something only he was able to enjoy. I couldn't wait until it was over.

I laid on the bed, as he handled his business. When he was about to cum, he grabbed my hair and went faster, making my ass jiggle more than it already was. I heard him in the back saying, "Look at that ass, baby, look at that ass! That big, fat, round, pretty ass!" I can't even lie, it turned me on a little. I knew for sure he busted my asshole wide open. After nutting in my asshole, he pulled out and fell straight to sleep.

The next day came, and I was leaving later on to go back home. That morning, Chris made me breakfast and brought it to me in bed, like he used to do. As I ate my breakfast, he laid next to me, hugging my waist and holding me tightly. When I was done eating, we had about six hours left to be together before I needed to head to the airport.

There was no telling when the next time would be that I would get laid, so, shit, I made the best of it while I could. Chris was lying on his back in the bed, making phone calls and textin' employees. So, I got up on my knees and topped him off with some sloppy. You know, that nasty, drooling, slippery head. He could hardly talk on the phone, so shortly after I started, he hung up.

I could tell he loved it. He moaned, he grabbed me, pushed my head how he wanted it and the entire time I did it, his toes curled. He started rubbing on my ass and then rubbed and squeezed my cat. As I swallowed him, I threw my legs across his head and covered his face with my pussy.

We went for a while, before he pulled me up and slid me down his body for me to sit on his dick. I did it as he wanted me to, slid it in and rode him like I was a certified porn star. We switched positions frequently, which included one of my favorites: doggy style. Chris knew how much I loved it when he hit it from the back.

We went for two rounds, before we went to wash. I loved having sex with Chris. He was a beast! He always pleased me, always, but make-up sex was always the best. Made me think I should be angry for no reason just to get fucked!

We laid down for the last hour before I had to leave and just talked. We had a heart to heart about our relationship. At that time, I took the opportunity to mention marriage counseling. He actually agreed to it, with no hesitation. He even told me he thought about that and wanted to mention it to me. He said when he came home, he would stay home for a while and we could focus on us, work things out and try to make it what it used to be. That's exactly what I wanted to hear! Maybe my life was coming together after all.

Chapter 14

"The Ultimate Betrayal"

Chris took me to the airport, but I didn't want to leave him. He told me he was comin' home soon, but when I asked him when, he couldn't give me an answer. I didn't understand it! If he missed his family and wanted to be with us, why not leave with me? Sometimes, I just didn't get the guy.

When I got to the airport, I sat for almost two hours; there was a delay in my flight. Then, after sitting there for an hour more, they told me that my flight was cancelled. I was ready to get home to my baby! I hadn't seen her in days and I needed to take care of some things at the shop. Once again, my plans were all fucked up.

When Chris dropped me off, he told me he was headin' to the club for an hour or two and that he would call me once he closed up and got home and settled. It was three hours since he left me. It was now almost midnight, so I didn't want to wake him if he was sleep or distract him if he was workin'. He didn't call or text me, so I figured he was busy. With that being said, I decided to take an Uber to the house to get some rest and relax until the morning.

I pulled up to the house and saw Chris' car home. I saw a light on in the house. It looked like a bathroom light, but there was no movement. Ok, cool, maybe he was asleep. He left the light on all the time. When I went in the house, I heard noise, but it was the TV. He always had the TV loud, as if he was a 65-year-old man with hearing aids. I went upstairs in the bedroom, opened the door and there my husband was, fuckin' the shit out of the same bartender that gave me the side-eye the day before.

He was fuckin' her just as good as he fucked me, and to put the icing on the cake, it was from the back - like I liked it. When I swung the room door open and saw that, my head started spinning. My jaw locked up and I blacked out. When he saw me, he was shocked. He stopped but was still inside her. He stood there and stared at me with a puzzled look on his face. Lookin' dumbfounded, like he normally did when he got caught doin' something wrong.

He was fuckin' this bitch who knew he was married, in my house, and in my bed. Fuckin' her disrespectfully on the sheets I nutted on just hours ago. He didn't even have the decency to change them before bringing her in. It had me wondering who else had nutted on those sheets I laid on. I was disgusted. I wasn't gone 24 hours yet and he was already on to the next bitch!

I started charging at her, first. I went to that bitch and I grabbed her by the hair. I dragged her off the bed and started pounding her face. Chris couldn't stop me. I kneed her in the face a few times, her nose started bleeding, but that didn't stop me. I had no mercy for that bitch. She disrespected me, so I gave her what she deserved. Shockingly, I did a damn good job, as I never was a fighter and fought only twice my whole life.

I eventually let her loose and Chris grabbed me by one arm. With the other, I knocked shit off the nightstand, tryin' to get ahold of the lamp. I finally got the lamp in my hand, Chris tried grabbing it from me, but it was too late. It had already hit her in the back of the head.

He took me downstairs to try and calm me. He let me loose, as he talked. Not listening to a word he was saying, I charged back up the stairs. There she was, still sitting on the floor, holding her face, crying.

"Oh, so you're still here? You want more, huh? It's best you get your shit and get the fuck out my house! I mean now, damnit," I hollered.

When I told her that, she started grabbing her uniform and rushing out the house, as she tried to put her clothes on. She almost fell down the stairs. Good thing she did it on her own, because I was attempted to push her myself. I didn't care about her. She wasn't my bitch, she was Chris's bitch. A fired one at that! She was out the door, now it was time for me to deal with his nasty-ass!

We were in the kitchen. Before I charged at him, I just looked at him, walking towards him slowly, without saying a word. He looked frightened. He had never seen me so angry. I never got this mad.

He didn't know what I was going to do next. Truth was, I didn't know what I was going to do next. I wasn't thinking! I didn't care what I did to him. Showing sympathy to him right now was out of the question. I couldn't care about his feelings, when he didn't give a damn about mine. If he had done so, this wouldn't be happening right now. I kept walking towards him. The closer I got, the more he backed up.

When I got by the sink, I opened the drawer and slammed it closed. For no reason at all, but to scare him more. I grabbed things off the counter and threw it at him. Once I was left with nothing on the counter to throw, I reached in the closest drawer to me and started grabbing things. I threw some spoons, I threw some forks, and the last thing I grabbed was a knife. Before I knew it, my hand was cocked back with the knife in it and released from my hand. It went towards Chris. It hit him in the hand. And right before my eyes, blood covered the floor.

Chris looked at me and yelled, "You…you bitch!" Right before he started breathing heavily and hollered in pain.

I had never done anything like it before. I hardly ever argued with men, let alone stabbing one. I was scared myself! I didn't know what to do! I wanted to call 911 and comfort him, but what if I went to jail? I had a kid, a business and a home to take care of! Jail was the last place I wanted to be.

I paced back and forth, with my hands on my head. Crying and panicking more and more, as the blood got thicker on the floor. I knew I had to think and act fast. I went over to Chris and asked him if he was ok. He said he was fine, he was just in a lot of pain and wanted me to take him to the hospital ASAP.

"What if they ask what happened? Are you going to tell them the truth? I don't see why you would, when you haven't been doing that any other time."

"I'll figure it out, Tara. I don't wanna hear yo' shit right now, just please, please get me to a hospital," he cried.

So, I ran around, trying to find my purse, Chris keys and something decent for Chris to put on. The entire drive to the hospital I was shaking. I was a nervous wreck. I kept checking on him to make sure he was still alive, as if I shot him in the chest or some sort. It was all him and that bum-ass bartender's fault. They should have never messed around.

When we got to the hospital, they grabbed him, and he explained what happened. I tortured that man all night, probably ruined it with him and his side bitch, and we were still on bad terms with each other; I knew for sure he wasn't going to look out for me and lie to make sure I was good.

When they asked him, he actually gave them a soft story about how he was cooking and somehow the knife jabbed him in the hand. What a lame-ass lie, right? I didn't give a damn, though, as long as I was good. I sat there and watched him put on a show and lie to the staffs' face, so I knew he'd done that to me before. They took him to get surgery on his hand, and about three hours later, we left the hospital and went back to the house.

The entire ride back home, I was still in a bad mood. I couldn't forget the reason why we were leaving the hospital in the first place. I bickered with Chris and argued about him fucking an employee. I was still unsettled about the situation. He told me he would get rid of her, but I didn't believe him.

He was really upset when I fucked my ex when we technically weren't together yet, but he was fucking his employee in the middle of our marriage. I felt like we were even. He gave me so much shit about that. I couldn't let him off easy.

When we got to the house, I was skeptical about sleeping there. I couldn't catch my flight back for a few more hours and I was exhausted. I didn't want to stay in the house with him. I wasn't sleeping in the bed with him, for sure, but I also didn't want to spend money on a hotel for just a few hours when I had a home much more comfortable and available to me. After thinking long and hard, I decided to stay at the house, but I slept in another room.

As I laid in that house, I started thinking about all that happened. I couldn't believe he really fucked that girl. How disrespectful! I mean, it was the ultimate betrayal! I couldn't believe it. Not Prince Charming who didn't do anything wrong!

I guess that was my karma! I guess it had to happen to me for me to see how it really felt. What he did was worse, though. Nothing could compare to the level he took it to. If that was his revenge, he won!

When Chris dropped me off at the airport later that day, I didn't speak to him on the ride there. Still hurt and disappointed, I decided not to hug or kiss him either. I was disgusted, knowing he would actually do something so horrendous, that I didn't want to touch him.

As I sat in the airport, he blew my phone up, but I didn't answer. Not one call! I was ready to get back home. That was my only concern.

When I landed in Charlotte and walked through the airport, guess who stopped me? The same fine-ass guy who was at the bowling alley the night we all went bowling. He said hi and told me how nice it was to see me again. I forgot I didn't have my ring on and he acknowledged that as well. He was still fine as hell, and me running into him was right on time. Look at God! I was so pissed about what Chris had done, that I decided to take his number this time. What's conversation when my husband was bangin' other chicks? He gave me a soft, tight hug and we went our separate ways... for now.

When I was getting into the Uber to go home and get my car, my phone rang. It was Gracie. She called me and told me to come to the shop as soon as I could. I headed over to the shop and when I got there, she told me she had some bad news.

I swear when my life was good, it was really good, but when it was bad, it seemed to be the worst shit ever. When I walked in, everything looked and seemed fine. The building was still standing, merchandise was still there, so I figured, oh... it can't be that bad.

Even if all my employees had quit, I could still manage. She told me, as she looked at my numbers, it was lookin' bad. We were definitely making money, but there was some missing as well. My eyes got really big. Somebody was stealing from me! The one person that looked out for everybody and made sure they were straight? Oh, hell naw! The first thing I did was call Chanel. Before Gracie came in, she was in charge of all of that. "Chanel, we need to talk ASAP! Come to the shop."

"Is everything good," she asked.

"We'll discuss it when you get here."

"I'm on my way."

We sat there digging into everything for almost two hours, as we waited for Chanel to show up, just to be sure we weren't making any mistakes of our own, or making an ass of ourselves. We realized that $20,000 went missing in the last three months. That's excessive! I didn't know how I didn't catch that. She was really good at what she did, I guess. When she arrived, I was so pissed, I still needed time to cool off before speaking, so Gracie started the conversation off.

"Hey, Chanel, Tara brought you in because she wanted to talk to you about something we discovered a few hours ago," Gracie told Chanel.

"And what might that be," Chanel asked, in a sassy voice.

"Twenty thousand dollars is missing! What do you have to say about that," I chimed in, asking Chanel.

"Well, what does that have to do with me? I didn't know anything about that and I damn sure didn't take it," Chanel replied.

"I never said you did, but how the hell you don't know anything about it, Chanel? It's your job to keep an eye on these things and take care of it! So, are you telling me now that you weren't doing your job properly," I asked.

"Wow! So, are you saying that I stole from you, Tara," Chanel asked.

"You were the only one with access to this! If you didn't, you know who did," I replied.

"I wasn't the only fuckin' manager you had! You need to check your damn sister or this bougie bitch! After all I've done for you, Tara? You think I would steal from you? Really," Chanel continued on.

"Pull that shit with somebody else. In the timeframe the money is missing, Michelle wasn't here," I said, shutting her down.

I continued, "After all I've done for you, Chanel, I can't believe it myself! This is way beyond what's accepted here in this boutique and it will not be tolerated. I'm suspending you without pay, until I get to the bottom of this."

"Fuck the suspension, don't even bother! I quit," Chanel said, loudly, as she walked out the office and slammed the door behind her.

"Wow," Gracie said.

"She really went overboard," I told Gracie.

I went on, "This is getting to be too much! I had the craziest weekend and now this bullshit. She was acting like she took it for real."

"Well, what happened," Gracie asked, and I wished she never did.

I gave her the rundown of what went on and told her that I also ran into the cute guy from the bowling alley. She tried to convince me to delete his number, but I refused. It was time I had some fun. I didn't want anything personal with the guy. I just wanted a cool-ass friend to kick it with. No sex, no strings attached and no drama.

Gracie told me to take some time to myself. She said she would handle things at the shop, and if she really needed me, she would call me. I was cool with that. I needed that break. When I went to pick up my kid, I swung by Chanel's, but she wasn't there. I tried calling her, but she didn't answer.

I knew she needed some time to cool off. I prayed it wasn't her stealing from me. I always looked out for her and gave her help, if I had it to offer. It would crush my heart to know she stole from me. I was losing everyone close to me. My sister, my husband and now my best friend.

Never in a million years did I think something like that would happen. We grew so close in the last few years. I knew for sure nothing could come between us and our bond. Man, if Mom was still here, I knew things would have been so much better. She was like the glue in the family. She kept everybody and everything together, no matter how tough the situation was.

I had so much going on. It seemed like one thing after another. Every time I was lifted, I was pulled back down. Every time I got a step ahead, I was dragged four steps back. I felt like I was losing myself. I felt like I didn't know who I was anymore. I needed to be at peace again.

It was time I was selfish. It was time I put myself before others and didn't care about anyone else's feelings or needs. It was clear that the ones I loved, and was willing to do whatever for, wasn't down for me like I was for them. Their loyalty for me didn't match the loyalty I had for them. I was being pushed away and hurt by the ones I loved most. I couldn't continue to go on like that.

Chapter 15

"The Start of Something New"

fter months of focusing on me, I felt refreshed. I was functioning better, worrying less about shit I couldn't change, and putting myself first - for once. I must say, it felt damn good! During those months, I isolated myself from as many people and problems as possible. I still didn't hear from Michelle and I was starting to adapt to it. I didn't talk to Chris and I was fine with that too. I didn't hear from Chanel either and I didn't bother reaching out anymore.

I noticed the change within myself. I felt the woman I had evolved into. Departing from the negativity helped tremendously, and I was happier than I'd been in a long time. Leaving my past in the past, I was excited about the start of something new.

A few days ago, I reached out to Anthony, the guy from the bowling alley. I called him, and he wanted to meet up, so I met him at a coffee shop. He was still the sweet, outgoing guy he was that night. He told me he still wasn't seeing anyone. Although I had no plans of being more than friends, I also didn't want to be dealing with some other chick's man either. That wasn't me.

I couldn't believe that his fine-ass was really single, but he told me he was single because the females he dealt with played too many games. Well, hell, the guys I came across were a piece of shit as well, so I could relate. I totally understood where he was coming from. I wasn't going to be naive that time, though. I was a broken woman. Words didn't mean shit to me, after dealing with two, sorry-ass niggas already that talked a good game. In due time, I would be introduced to the real him and see if what he talked was as real as he said it was. I wasn't falling victim anymore. Dealing with me wasn't gonna come easy like it did in the past.

We talked and laughed for maybe an hour before leaving. Before we parted ways, I asked him if he was on social media and he told me yeah. He gave me his Facebook, Snapchat and Instagram names. When I got in the car, I immediately looked him up.

I didn't send a friend request right away because I didn't want to make it obvious that I visited his pages so soon. After lurkin' on his Instagram and fantasizing over his sexy-ass pics, I went on his Facebook. I scrolled on his Facebook, and there were still no signs of him having a girl, baby, side chick, fuck friend or anything. Lookin' heavily, I ended up in some pictures he posted six months ago, and there I saw him in a pic with Josh. My mouth dropped.

"Damn!" I yelled, hitting my steering wheel hard. I was so damn disappointed!

How the hell did he know Josh? Did he know Chris too?

"Calm down, Tara. Breathe!" I told myself. I wanted to investigate and figure this shit out. Instead, I was like fuck it! I deserved to be happy! I caught my husband fuckin' another bitch. Even if he did know Chris, I didn't care. Besides, all we were having was conversation anyways. It wasn't like we were having sex.

As weeks went by, we talked more. I liked him and all, but I started to wonder if I was using him as a rebound to cover up my own wounds I was still healing from. I didn't want to talk to him to make Chris mad. But letting Chris see another man loving me wasn't a bad idea either. I wanted to show him what he was missin'. I didn't care about Chris' feelings anymore, and as time went on, I didn't care about our marriage or being with him either.

Breaking up our family was the only thing that bothered me. I didn't want to be responsible for that. I knew that little girl I carried for nine months would eventually hurt, as she got older, not having her dad around all the time. I've always had my dad, so I couldn't relate.

The cool thing about Anthony was he didn't have any kids. I didn't have to deal with any baby momma drama. I didn't have to worry about another bitch holding a baby over his head or using a baby to get him back. If I fucked with him on that level, he would be mine completely. I didn't have to share. The thought of that excited me.

One day I was chillin' with Anthony and he asked me about my marriage. He remembered running into me at the airport without my ring, and months later I still wasn't wearin' it. I didn't know how to tell him that I was still married - technically. I never wanted to let another guy in on my business, but I had to let him know what it was. Although we were just friends, I felt we should still be able to be open with one another… no matter what.

I spilled it. I told him I was still married, but that we were separated for a while. I told him how I wanted to make it work until I caught him fuckin' another bitch in our bed. I also told him how I flipped out and what I did to Chris, so he didn't think once about taking advantage of this pretty-ass, innocent face. I had to let him know when shit get sour, I could turn into a savage. He ended up showing more interest in me, after finding out I was a crazy bitch. He wasn't trippin' about me still being married; it brought me even closer to him.

He was a really cool guy, but so was Norris and Chris in the beginning. I was still hurt from Norris but gave Chris a chance. I was currently hurting from Chris, and if it came down to it, I wanted to be able to give him a chance; but deep down inside, I was still scared. It was a cycle I couldn't break free from. I had a guard up when it came to men now. Eventually, I would want to be able to let it down, but I wasn't ok with getting hurt again.

Anthony also had his own place and was working in a lawyer's office for his extern. He would be graduating college soon as a Criminal Law Attorney. He took care of his elderly grandma and she lived with him. He didn't have much, but that didn't change how I felt about him, as long as he wasn't coming off as a gold digger.

He had a rough life; his mom abandoned him and his brothers. His grandma stepped in and raised them. His brothers were in the streets and he didn't trust them looking after his grandma, so he took on the responsibility. He did it with the help of home health nurses. He was churchgoing. He went every Sunday, faithfully, with his grandma.

He had a fun sense of humor and always said how he felt, good or bad. I already told myself I was going to take things slow with him, learn who he was, and develop a friendship and bond before dating him, but clearly, he wanted me sooner than I was willing to give myself to him. It was flattering, though… Him being all over me and shit. Sometimes, a girl needed that.

Anthony asked me what I was doing the following day because he wanted to see me. I told him I would be at the boutique and to call me when he was on the way. He still didn't know where I lived, and I didn't want to invite him over to a house that Chris and I shared. That was total disrespect to me, even if we weren't together. When Armani got put to bed, I laid in the bed next to her on the phone with him. While we talked, I searched online for condos. Moving out of this house was my final step to movin' on.

I wanted to be away from everyone. I didn't want anyone to know where I lived. I wanted to get out of this damn house that Chris' spirit was in. Being in that house put me in a bad mood, at times. I would sage the house from time to time, but that still didn't work. Now that I was moving on, it was time for a new home, leaving all the old shit that involved him behind.

The next day came and I woke up to someone ringing my doorbell. Chris was in Atlanta, Anthony didn't know where I stayed, and Gracie was at the boutique, getting ready to open up. Those were the only people I expected to show up on my doorstep. *Who could it be?* I wasn't expecting anyone. I got up to open the door and guess who it was? Chanel.

"Hey! I wasn't expecting you. What's up," I asked her, as I cracked the door with half of my body in it.

We hadn't spoken in months. She was still suspect about a lot of shit, and since she quit the boutique, I really hadn't been fuckin' with her. I couldn't let her in! In fact, I had my mind made up that I wasn't.

"Can I come in," she asked.

"Uh… no, you may not, Chanel! I haven't spoken to you in months. You pop up to my house without running it by me first, and last time I saw you, you stormed out the store when I told you that you were suspended. Then, you quit on me! So, like I asked, what's up," I said, with a firm voice and a straight face.

I was serious. I got straight to the point. As I worked on myself to become a better person, I refused to entertain negativity and bullshit. She stood on my doorstep and her smile turned upside down really quick when I said that.

"So, I have to run it by my best friend before coming to her house when I never had to do that before," she asked, with a stupid-ass look on her face.

"Yes, you are absolutely right," I told her.

Then I went on to clear more shit up. "I don't even know if I'm your best friend anymore. I should hope not, because the shit you did to me, best friends don't do to each other. Not real best friends, at least. Not a best friend who practically was a sister. Not a best friend who I loved and trusted, but hurt me to my core. Back in the day when I could trust you, you could show up to my house, but now that things have changed between us, it's unacceptable at this point!"

"Wow! Ok, Tara. You've said how you felt. Cool."

"Yes, I have and that's not all, actually! I wish you would speak on where my 20 bands went and when I'm getting it back!" I told her.

"So, it's all about money with you? Is that what it is? Money is everything to you, right," she went on to say.

I started to get angry. I stepped outside the door and closed the door behind me, as I had a feeling the conversation was going to blow up. She had some nerve to say it's all about money when she knew it's never been that way. Twenty bands don't come easy. If I gave it to her, it was one thing, but to steal it from me was something different. I don't respect that shit...at all! That bitch was silly. I was somewhat happy we fell out. The Chanel that stood on my doorstep, I no longer knew.

I got up in her face and told her, "To set the record straight, it's never been about the money and you know that! It's the principal. I've looked out for you before I had all of this. When I pretty much had nothing. I don't understand why you couldn't come to me and ask. Instead, you took from me, and because of that, I can't trust you. If I can't trust you, I can't fuck with you, period. Yes, I do want my money. It's $20,000, Chanel! Who wouldn't want it back? Not once have you come to me and apologized."

"It's all good, Tara! Do your thing. You don't have to fuck with me! It hurts that you would treat me like this, but like they say, friends come and go! Just because you looked out for me, don't think I need you! I can do bad by myself and I will be on top," Chanel said to me and walked off.

She was driving a car I had never seen before. It wasn't the one I gave her, for sure. *That's probably where my $20,000 went*, I thought.

She never said why she showed up to my house. I wondered why she even came. I refused to call and ask, though. I was done making peace with people that did me wrong. Nobody would ever understand how bad I wanted to choke her ass out and leave her lying on the stone in front of my door.

Not letting that bitch ruin my day, I left the house, after getting dressed. I'd spoken to Anthony on my way to the boutique and he told me he would be out and about. He wanted to see me, even if it was just for a few minutes. I told him he could swing by the boutique and to let me know when he arrived, so I could come outside. He said, "ok" and then hung up.

When I got to the boutique, Gracie was already there. I was talking with her and I told her what happened, as I got on the floor to rearrange merchandise and stock.

"She had some nerve showing up without permission," Gracie said.

"That's what I said! You know I hadn't seen or heard from her since we all were in the office, right," I told Gracie.

In the middle of our conversation, Gracie asked, "Are you expecting someone, Tara?"

When I turned around toward the door, Anthony was standing right in front of the glass, in the open for everyone to see. I told him to let me know when he was out there. Instead, he decided to stand in front of the glass with flowers in one hand and food in the other.

That was what I didn't want him to do. I didn't want everyone in my business. I didn't want everyone knowing who I was dealing with. Damn! Niggas just don't listen. When people know who you're dealing with, unnecessary bullshit arises. I wanted us to be low-key and chill privately.

"Yes, I'm expecting him!" I said, explaining to her that he was my friend.

I welcomed him in the shop. When he walked in, Gracie recognized him and called him by his name. I somewhat expected that, because I saw him in a picture with Josh.

I showed him around, as we walked in the back to my office.

"The place is nice," he told me.

It seemed like he knew that I was annoyed at the fact that he didn't listen to what I told him to do. It was like he was distracting me with compliments and it was somehow working. Thank God he brought food too because I was hungry as hell.

Eating lunch and talking to him didn't feel right. I didn't know if it was my guilt of still being married, or if it was because I really wasn't feelin' him. He was into me. He had already told me multiple times that he wanted me, but I was still focused on building a friendship. I wanted time to myself before being tied down again. I didn't want to jump from one relationship to another, not allowing myself to enjoy what the single life had to offer.

When he left, Gracie came to me.

"I can't believe that's who you're dealing with."

"He is just a friend. Why did you say it like that, though? What do you know about him," I asked, curiously.

"Nothing much, really. I think Josh knows him or of him. They've been around each other," Gracie said.

"Oh ok! He was the guy trying to hit on me at the bowling alley that was with those dudes that night. Do you remember?"

"It was dark, and I was drunk, I don't remember, girl."

"Blind as a bat," I joked with her, as we both laughed.

"How does Josh know him?" I asked.

"I think Josh is friends with a couple of his cousins and from being around his cousins he got to know Anthony. I don't think Chris knows them, though. If he does, it's not like how Josh knows them," she threw in there.

"My last concern is Chris. I'm focused on my happiness," I told her.

"Good for you and I don't blame you! You are an amazing wife, amazing mom and, overall, an amazing person! You deserve all the good that comes to you!"

I thanked her for that and gave her and the baby growing in her stomach a big hug!

"I have one request, though," I told her.

"What may that be," she replied.

"Let's just keep Anthony and I between us. Just for now, and not because of Chris. Just because you know what could happen if too many people get into your relationship too soon."

"Yeah, I get it. That's fine! My lips are sealed! If anyone asks, I know nothing," Gracie said.

Although I was moving on, there were still some things holding me back. I still loved Chris, without a doubt. I was committed to the vows we shared. I didn't want anyone but my husband. I was still torn, though. I was indecisive about if I actually wanted to leave him or not. Should I stay, or should I go?

I found myself askin' that over and over again. Catching him banging another bitch's brains out, in our own home, less than 24 hours after fucking me, was making a fool of me. All of those things wasn't even the half of why I should walk away from the marriage.

Was it all something I could get pass and move on from? The answer to that question, I wasn't sure of. I knew if I tried, it would play over and over again in my head. The image, her moans, the things he said to her. There was no way our relationship would ever be the same afterwards.

In the back of my mind, movin' on was the smartest choice I could make. I knew speeding up the moving process and selling the home would help me forget about him too. I needed to stop loving and caring about him like I did. I also felt like I needed to lose hope that we would be able to be what we once were.

Maybe havin' Anthony in my life was not a bad thing. Especially, if he stayed the person he portrayed himself to be. I was still going to take it slow, though. Keeping busy would definitely get Chris off my mind. I still hadn't spoken to him in a while, and I refused to call.

I started going harder with the hunt for a new home. I found another condo, even better than the first one I had, and it was available for immediate occupancy. I went to do everything I could with the realtor. It took about three weeks for everything to be processed and I moved in the following weekend.

I was beyond excited. The vibe was different, the smell was different, how I felt in my home was different, the happiness that filled my heart was different, the way I felt as a woman in the new place was different. That was what I needed.

When I moved in, guess who I invited to help me unpack? Yep, Anthony, of course. Chris didn't know where I stayed, or when I moved. He didn't know anything about my new place and I planned to keep it that way. Besides, I wasn't his girl. At

Courtney Simone

least that's how he made it seem. So, I'm sure I was the last chick on his mind anyway.

We got a good bit of the house unpacked and we were hungry, so I ordered delivery from a Chinese restaurant. We sat in the living room and ate, while watching TV. It was a real chill day. Normally, I liked to be in bed while watching movies, but I wanted to take it slow with him. How crazy my sex drive was, if we went in the bedroom, I knew for sure I would have ended up fuckin' him. I loved having sex! I couldn't control it, sometimes; especially, around a fine-ass nigga. Somehow, I always found myself with one, which resulted in me fuckin' them shortly after meeting them. With Anthony, I wanted to do things differently, this time.

I always felt like having sex too soon ruined a good relationship. I had my mind set on doing things differently, hoping for a better outcome. Besides, Anthony was already all over me. If I gave him some pussy, the dude would be stalking me. He knew where I lived now; he even knew where I worked. The power of my pussy would probably have him holding baby Armani hostage. I couldn't give it up to him… not this soon. You know what they say; anything worth having is worth waiting for. When it came to me, that shit was definitely real.

Chapter 16

"Where Do We Stand"

About a week went by, and with all the moving, I really hadn't had time to clean the house that I left. I took some time out of my day to go over and do some light cleaning, just before grabbing the last bit of things I wanted. As I was heading over to the house, I got a call.

"Hello?" I said.

"Hey! What's up? Are you busy? Do you have a minute?"

"That's all I have, actually! What's up?"

"I know we haven't talked much since you left, and I wanted to sit down and explain, apologize and see what we can do to make things work."

It was Chris. He must be out of his damn mind. He was just hitting me up after all that time. Again, he never asked about or mentioned his daughter. I wasn't impressed with the way he even started the conversation. I was already hesitant about answering, but I was curious to know why he was calling, so, I did.

When I was still interested in us, he was focused on other bitches. Now that I was out, he wanted his family back. After I practically begged him to come back home, he stayed and did what he wanted to do. Things must have not worked out in

Atlanta like he thought it would. Or maybe he wanted to do things on his terms, but my daughter and I weren't available.

Sitting down with him would be difficult. Although I stabbed him in the hand, that wasn't all I wanted to do. Sitting in his face would really make me want to slap him as hard as I could, bust his lip, black his eye, bloody his nose, and even choke the hell out of him. It would definitely be challenging, but I deserved answers; and most importantly, an apology.

He was in town, so I told him to come to the house. Little did he know, the place we once shared was no longer my home. I was upstairs, cleaning, when he walked in.

"Tara," Chris yelled, as his voice echoed.

"I'm coming down!"

"So, what's this all about," he asked me.

"I moved out. What does it look like? I'm glad you're here because I want to talk to you about selling the place."

"Why?"

"What do you mean 'why'? You're not here, I'm not here and we're moving on. What's the purpose of keeping it?"

"Wow… I knew you didn't want me, but I wasn't expecting all of this to happen so soon!"

"Well, you are in Atlanta living it up! Living your best life, and living in this house was depressing. I couldn't stay anymore. I wanted to do the same. I needed to move out. I'm moving on from all of this!"

His jaw dropped, when I told him that. Me moving on was the last thing he wanted to hear. Especially, when he showed up to talk about us working things out.

"I came here to talk to you about rekindling what we had, and bettering our relationship. I want my wife back! I want my family back!"

I wanted to laugh in his face. Everything he said went in one ear and out the other. It was all bullshit! Back in the day, I had a soft, gooey, warm heart. After being taken advantage of time and time again, I couldn't fall for the lies I was fed. It didn't satisfy my appetite anymore.

"It's funny that you came here to talk to me about getting me back, but not once have you mentioned Armani. You haven't checked on her in months. You haven't provided for her in months. Do you really think I would be interested, or even give you another chance, when you are a fuckin' deadbeat? That shit turns me off. I can't call you my husband, nor can I lay up with a man who doesn't do right by his kid. I'm better than that! No way in hell you could even think that this is right. You want me, but don't give a fuck about my child. How does that work,Chris? Please, explain it to me!"

"You're right, baby...and I'm sorry! That's why I want us to be back together, under one roof, so I can be a better father."

He cried out to me, as he tried to grab me by the waist, pulling me closer to him.

Although his sex was good, and his dick was big, I didn't want him near me. He disgusted me - still. I didn't know how many more girls he had been in, after the one I caught him with. I didn't want anything to do with him.

I pulled away, held my composure and continued on with what I needed to say.

"So, let me get this clear. You are tellin' me that you have to be with me to be involved in your child's life? Are you telling me that you have to be in the home to provide and show her love? If that's the case, you are a sorry-ass man! You can dismiss yourself now! You wanna know what's also fucked up, Chris? I believed in you. I took a chance with you, when I was still brokenhearted by another motherfucker who took my love for granted and played me. I thought you were the sweet, little, innocent Prince Charming I always dreamt about and knew I deserved. I thought you was coming to sweep me off my feet and show me different; but instead, you turned out to be the same as what I've dealt with before! A sorry-ass nigga!"

I stopped to let him speak, but realized I wasn't done.

"You are a manipulative son of a bitch! You were real smooth, let me tell you that! You called me the slut, but in reality, you are! You called me the cheater, but you are! You called me the ho, but, motherfucker, you are! What I did was before you. Not once have I stepped out on my marriage! Obviously, the vows we exchanged meant nothing to you."

I continued, "You hurt me worse than any man did! You hurt my daughter and she doesn't even know it. You did me dirty, Chris. I can't do this anymore!"

He got furious. He started walking around the house, slapping and boxing walls. He was huffing and puffing. He started mumbling under his breath. All I could think about was, *there goes that demon again.* It felt like déjà vu when we had that big blowup before. There we were, standing in the living room, again, where it all happened. Only difference was, the place was empty, and I was so much stronger - mentally.

As bad as I wanted to try and hurt him physically, like he did me, I didn't. Watching him walk around as angry as he was frightened me. He walked up to me and I wanted to punch him before he did it to me. Not knowing what he had in his mind to do, I prayed he didn't lay hands on me again.

"I've tried to be patient with you. I've tried to look at the bigger picture and forget about the possibility of this child not being mine. We still haven't taken a DNA test and this situation is being ignored. Still, here you are, throwin' it in my face about me not being there for Armani, when her ass might not even be mine!"

Wow… he really came out and said a child that may not be his. It seemed to me like this was some shit he wanted to say for a long time now. After all he said to me, when I was in Atlanta that last time, I was shocked to hear him say that. This was the same person that said he wanted to be there for us no matter what.

I knew he was full of shit. I knew the things he told me was just being said because he felt like that's what I wanted to hear. The truth was finally coming out.

"Obviously, that's how you've felt deep down for a while. Since you are being honest, I have some things I would like for you to address - *honestly*. Even if it fuckin' kills you," I told him.

"Tell me how long you've been fuckin' your employee. Tell me if that's the only person you've fucked while dealin' with me. Tell me if you love her... if you fucked her since I kicked her ugly-ass out. Tell me if you fired the bitch, like you said you would. Tell me if you enjoyed fucking her…if you prefer another bitch over me. Tell me whose chocolate syrup that really was," I yelled to him, as I started crying.

He stood there, with one hand on his chin. I could tell I hit him below the belt and those weren't things he wanted to address at that time. He wasn't ready to answer, I could tell. Hell, I wasn't ready to hear the shit he was getting ready to say. I needed that closure, though. This was the truth I'd been waiting on for a long time.

"So, is this it between us," Chris asked me, instead of giving me answers.

"Can you tell me what I deserve to know? How could you turn this on me? Answer the fucking questions," I hollered.

He could tell I was beyond pissed. The echo that added to my voice even intimidated me. He knew I wasn't there for fun and games. If he didn't answer the questions I asked the next time he opened his mouth, that day would also be the last day he saw or heard from me.

He stood there in silence for a while, just looking at me, as he contemplated how he was going to answer those questions. I stood there along with him, impatiently waiting for the answers I already knew. There was silence for a while, and then he finally opened his big-ass mouth.

"Ok, here goes. I haven't spoken to her, since the night all of that happened. I don't love her either. She was just a fling. Something I could hit and get head from when I wanted to. She didn't mean shit to me. Only reason she was at the house was because I didn't want to spend money on a room," Chris said, but I interrupted him with more questions.

"So, you mean to tell me, you would rather disrespect me because you'd rather be cheap? It was one thing to be fuckin' this girl, but it's another to be fuckin' her in our home, in our damn bed, not even 24 hours after parting ways with me. Damn! You didn't even have the decency to wait a while. That's cold, Chris! So, tell me this. Was she the only person you've been fuckin', Chris?"

He got quiet, again, and I immediately knew that was a no.

"It's not, Tara, and I've been dealing with one person, in particular, almost the entire time we've been married."

When Chris said that, I almost lost it. I almost flipped out. I wanted to stab him, again, but that time, in his heart, on purpose, like he just did to me. Maybe it was best that we met up for this conversation in an empty home.

Deep down, I already knew the answers to the questions I asked. I knew he had more to tell. I knew he had yet to answer all the questions I asked, but I couldn't take it anymore. Tears filled my eyes more than ever before. I was still young. I was only married for a couple years, and the husband I thought was my everything, turned out to be everything I didn't want in a man at all.

It hurt me so bad to know I was being played for years. I was told lies, straight to my face, for years. I had been intimate with a guy who was giving his loving to other women for years. I thought I could trust him. I thought he loved me, but I had to face reality that he never did. He played victim so many times and acted innocent. There was nothing innocent about this dude. He did more to me than he could ever say I'd done to him. Unless you have been hurt like I have, you would never understand my pain.

I couldn't even explain it. My heart was heavy! My eyes were filled with tears, and my head thumped in pain. I needed to get away from him. Before we met, before he came or even contacted me, I was working on myself. I wanted to move on, but I was still hesitant about it. I knew for sure I was done, this time. It was too much. Chris had real problems he needed to fix within himself. I don't think he even loved himself. There was no way he could love me and my daughter the way we deserved to be loved.

He stood on his side and I stood on mine. I gave him a vicious look. So many thoughts of ways I wanted to hurt this man ran across my mind. I started to blackout, again. I was never that way before dealing with him. That's how I knew he was no good for me.

"Tara? Tara!" He called my name multiple times.

I heard him, but it was faint. My mind was in another state. He came up to me and grabbed me by the waist. He should have never done that. I didn't want him talking to me, let alone touching me. When he did that, I snapped!

I started twisting and turning, while I swung my arms, hitting him.

"Get off of me! Get the fuck off of me!" I yelled, and I hollered, as I continued to cry. Don't touch me! You are a...I don't know what the hell you are. I know that you are disgusting. I don't want you near me. Leave me alone, Chris. Just leave me alone...forever!"

"Tara, baby, please! Let me at least apologize!"

"Fuck your apology, Chris. It means nothing to me like I mean nothing to you."

"I just want you to know that I love you and I always have. I'm not proud of what I've done. I want help. I want to be with you. I can't live without you. You are everything I want and need in a woman. Everything about you turns me on. I love you, baby. I need you. I'll do whatever it takes to get you back. Please, don't leave me! I'm begging you."

Chris was on his knees crying. Him on his knees meant nothing to me. The tears that rolled down his cheeks meant nothing to me. I didn't care. I couldn't care. He turned my heart to where I could spit in his face, while he was down there shedding tears. I was done! It was fucked up that I would have to be a single mom, but I was already doing it. It was fucked up that I was so young and possibly facing a divorce, but life goes on.

While Chris was on his knees, crying and making a fool of himself, I walked right out the door; on my way out, I slammed the door behind me. I wanted him to know how little him being down on the floor, begging for me back, meant to me. Fuck him! Although he and Norris had done me wrong, I wasn't ready to give up on love completely.

Thankfully, I found out everything when I did. I was thankful I still had my whole life ahead of me. I held on to the faith that I would come across a guy who would treat me like the queen I am. Who would appreciate me for what I did and didn't do. Who would be solid with me and never switch up. I knew he would come at the right time, and I was willing to be patient.

Sooner or later, he would regret losing me and doing everything he did to me. He would understand that I was as loyal as they come. He would realize that he can find another woman, but not one who would love him and treat him as good as I did. With no hate towards him, I wanted him to eventually be happy. I prayed that he got his life together and changed. I just wasn't willing to stick around to see if it was possible, or if it was actually going to happen.

Chapter 17

"Movin' On"

As I faced the fact that my husband was an actual asshole, the $20,000 that was stolen from me was still on my mind. It wasn't a loss I was willing to take, so I decided to get a lawyer. It was sad it had to get to that point, but I gave Chanel many chances. I was willing to work with her on paying me my money back, but since she wanted to be a bitch about it, that was no longer an option.

My family and I helped her out for most of her life. She didn't work for me any longer, and I doubted she had another job, so I didn't know how she would be able to pay me my money back. That wasn't my concern, though. I was leaving it in the hands of a judge. I didn't tell anyone I was taking that route, not even Gracie. I planned on keeping it that way, but once Chanel found out, I knew everyone else would too.

Days went by since I had last spoken to Anthony. He was calling and texting me, but I ignored him. I knew he was worried. Thankfully, he didn't pop up at my house or he would have been on my shit list too. He'd been really good about falling back, lately, though.

I stayed home for days, ignoring everybody and everything. I stayed home and chilled with the little person who made me the most happy - my baby girl. Spending quality time with her, without interruptions, felt amazing. It made me wonder how life would be as a mom if I didn't have to share my time with the boutique. I wondered how parenting would be if I had so much more time to spend with her.

At times, I felt guilty about not being with her as much as I would like, but there was always a good reason behind it. Unlike Chris, I didn't neglect my kid for niggas or bitches. I was still pissed about that. Every time I thought about it, it made me mad.

When I laid Mani down for a nap, I went to unpack some more to get my mind off things. After about an hour to myself, I called Anthony. He was glad to hear from me. He wasn't even upset because he knew I was probably busy.

The next day, I called Gracie to check on her and the boutique. As soon as I called her, she told me she was just about to call me. I couldn't figure out why she would be calling me, if everything was all good at the boutique and she wasn't in labor. She hardly ever called me when she was at the boutique. The only time she did was if something was really wrong. The last time she called me, it was when we found out about the $20,000 missing.

I didn't know if I was ready for more on my plate. I had enough I was dealin' with. Like I said before, if it's not one thing, it's another. Regardless, I would have to hear what she had to say, so I told her to go on and tell me.

She asked me if I had gotten any calls. People was calling me, but people always called me. I ignored calls for almost a week, so I didn't know what was going on. She went on and told me Ms. Sherlene passed away from breast cancer. My stomach turned multiple times.

She was just getting herself together and her life back on track. She was focused on being a better person for herself, Chanel and Norris. Ms. Sherlene was with me almost all my life.

Chanel and I became friends at a young age, so we watched each other grow. I could only imagine how Chanel and Norris felt. I'd already experienced the feeling of losing a parent. I lost both. It wasn't easy. She had to deal with all that, and now she would be getting served about the money she owed me.

Even though I wasn't fuckin' with Chanel, I felt her pain. Years were wasted with her not spending time with Ms. Sherlene, and shortly after she had a change in heart, she lost her. Ms. Sherlene was home with Mom and Dad now. It was fucked up how soon she left us, though.

Gracie was still on the phone. She asked me if I was ok, constantly. She knew the role that lady played in my life. When I gathered myself, Gracie told me a little more. She said, apparently, Ms. Sherlene knew she had breast cancer for a while, which was one reason she got help with her drug addiction.

She knew if she didn't get help, she wouldn't be able to be around her kids, which motivated her to do better. She wanted to fix things and be with them as much as she could because things weren't looking good for her. Chanel didn't find out that her mom had cancer until she was called to the hospital days before her mother died.

She didn't tell them she was sick because she didn't want them to feel sorry for her or treat her as if she was. She didn't want to worry them and have them stressin' over her situation. To make the situation worse, Norris was in jail.

He was convicted on drug charges. His drug dealing, and fast money had eventually caught up with him; it was just at a bad time. Gracie said he could get out, if someone could come up with $1000, but nobody had the money to get him out. She said Josh and his friends were looking to pitch in, but she didn't know what was going on with that. Everything was fucked up.

As bad as I wanted to call Chanel and send condolences and support to her, I couldn't. It hurt. I couldn't believe we were at that point in our lives, when we were so tight back in the day. We'd been through so much together. I didn't want to believe that I actually missed her, but truth was... I did.

Since Norris was in jail and nobody really had the bond money but me, I bailed him out. Norris and I hadn't been on the best of terms lately because he was doing slick shit after I started dating Chris. I couldn't believe I was saying this, but I needed him just as much as he needed me right now.

I was doing what was best for a friend, myself and my daughter. It wouldn't sit right with me, knowing he was in jail when his mom was being buried. Giving him the opportunity to be by Chanel's side and see his mom one last time meant everything. That pain would hurt so much different, if he wasn't able to.

The love Norris still had for me, he would do anything to be able to talk to me again and be in my presence. When I went down to bail him out, I had more than just feelings and thoughts, I also had tricks up my sleeves.

I waited for about two hours before Norris was released. The look on his face said a lot, when he saw me sitting there.

"Never thought you would be here doing this for me," he said.

"Well, it's for a good cause; now bring yo' ass on," I told him.

When we got in the car, there was awkward silence for a while. I was hesitant to ask what I needed to ask, unsure if it was the right time to do so. After about eight minutes of riding, Norris broke the silence.

"So, what made you do this for me?"

"Well, to be quite honest, I only put up half. I gave $500 while Josh, Steven, and Rocko came up with the other $500, so there's more people to thank besides me. The main reason I came was because of Ms. Sherlene. You couldn't be in jail while all of this was going on. The shit wouldn't be right. I've been in your shoes. I know how it feels. I don't know if you know, but Chanel and I had a major fallout, so unfortunately, I can't be there for her as I'd like to. You are all she really has and she needs you. Just to let you know, I'm not looking for you to pay me back. I just ask that you do one, huge favor for me."

"Would your husband accept this? How would he feel that you're here for me?"

As bad as I wanted to tell him don't worry about Chris' ass because I wasn't, I didn't. He didn't know what was going on between us and it really wasn't any of his business, so I kept it cool and ignored what he said.

"It's cool," I told him.

"What's the favor, though," Norris asked me.

"I want you to take a DNA test for our…" I stopped in my tracks and switched up my words. "…my baby girl." I shook my head. I couldn't believe that came out like that.

"So, how do you feel about doing it," I asked.

"I'll do it. There's no problem with that. I've wanted to know from the beginning. I don't have kids, and if she is mine, I want to be a part of her life. That's why I've been trying to be involved as much as I could. Just in case she was, you know? I didn't want to miss out on anything, but you thought I was on some bullshit. I don't know what took you so long to decide this," Norris told me.

I was speechless.

"Can I see a picture of her," Norris went on to ask me.

I was so shocked at how involved he really wanted to be. Protecting my marriage, I overlooked everything Norris was doing back then. As I sat there, hearing him out, I realized he didn't mean any harm. I was stuck so far up Chris' ass, I was pushing away a friend I always had.

I never doubted that Norris would be a good father. With no plans on us getting back together, I just prayed he wasn't. He really wasn't a bad person, he was just a man. A man who got into all the wrong shit and who couldn't commit himself to just one, bomb-ass female.

"Wow, she's beautiful. She looks just like me. My bad, I meant you," he joked, handing my phone back.

I laughed a little.

"I'm proud of you, Tara!"

I was thinking... like, *where is all this coming from? Why now? Is this a part of one of his sneaky-ass plans or was it genuine?* Sometimes, it was hard to tell with him. I just said thank you.

"No, for real, I really am! You have grown to be a beautiful, hard-working woman, a great mom, and you got a good heart... I'm proud of you! I'm happy you are my daughter's mother."

I looked at him, with my eyes wide open.

"What the hell you..." I started to ask Norris, and then he interrupted me.

"I already know, Tara, and you do too. I think you denied it because I hurt you. It was wrong, and it wasn't on purpose. You doubted me being her dad because you didn't want to run off your new man."

Norris was speaking facts. Chris wasn't going to stick around, if he knew what really went on. Norris knew me like no one else. Although he was right, I didn't respond to any of what he said. I just put my head down. He looked at me, grabbed my chin, lifted it and turned my face toward his.

"I know you, Tara! Since you were a little girl. I know what it is. I'm not going to hold you up much longer, so just call me when you're ready to go. Do you still have my number?"

"Yes, I have it, Norris!" I told him, as I grinned and cut my eyes at him.

"Thank you for everything. Can I get a hug," he asked.

I was hesitant, at first, but why not? We both got out the car and hugged each other.

He put his arms around my waist, his hands fell on my ass and I had no choice but to put my arms around his neck. He held me tightly. He lifted me off the ground, spun me around and said, "Ok, I quit." I wanted to tell him not to, but I behaved. When I got back in the car, he closed my car door behind me and watched me as I drove off.

Yeah, he really missed me. All this ass and good-ass pussy too! Ha ha! Hugging him for that two minutes made me miss him too. After all those years, feelings were still there and chemistry too. We lived totally different lives. I don't know if we could ever be together again. I wasn't willing to risk everything I had for the nonsense he had going on. I don't think he would change the life he lived to accommodate my wants and needs to make me happy. Never did I ever want to date a street nigga. Never did I think Norris would be one either.

Three days went by and it was time for the funeral. I contemplated on if I should take Armani with me or not, but I decided to take her. Gracie met me at my house and rode with me. We went to the church and it was very beautiful. Afterwards, we went to a center where the gathering and dinner was being held.

Josh, Steven, and Rocko were there. They all came over and spoke to the three of us. Josh took Mani and showed her off for a while. Norris played with her, while she was in Josh's arms. A few minutes after Josh brought her back to me, Norris came over to us. He hugged Gracie, hugged me and asked me if he could hold Mani. I gave him permission and he held her while standing next to me.

"Can we move, or do we have to stand here," he asked.

I told him he could take her, but I wanted them to stay where I could see her. I also told him, whatever he did, to not let Chanel hold my baby. I didn't care if it seemed petty; my kid, my rules.

Norris looked at me crazy, and then he whispered in my ear, "I will fulfill your request today, but once we take the test and it shows she is my kid, some arrangements will need to be made. That is my sister, making Chanel her aunt. Y'all need to work that shit out," and then he walked off.

He didn't even give me time to say what I wanted. All I could say to myself was, *damn*. I forgot that Chanel would be my child's aunt! How would that work? That was lots of drama alone. Gracie just looked at me, as she sipped her tea through her straw.

"I don't even want to know," she said to me, before I was able to say anything.

When I looked over to check on my baby, he had her walking while he held her hand. It was so damn cute, man. I started to think he would be a better father than Chris would. Chris had his life together and Norris didn't, which made it even crazier. You would think the opposite, right?

Two minutes later, I looked over and Norris had her in his arms, again. That wasn't the problem, though... Chanel was in their faces and she was talking, laughing and playing with my child. I didn't know how to feel. She wasn't holding her, as I requested. But, what made her think it was ok to be in my child's face when she didn't care for me?

I didn't approve of that. I told Gracie I would be back.

Gracie said, "No, Tara, please sit back down!"

I heard her, but I didn't listen. I got up, and as I was walking over to them, Norris was walking towards me. He was bringing Mani back. I didn't say anything to him about that. I just took my baby and went back to our table.

"Are you ready," I asked Gracie.

"Yeah, we can go, I'm tired anyways. Waiting on Josh, I'll be here all night."

I went over to Norris, and Gracie stepped over to talk to Josh.

"I'll meet you at the car," she told me.

"Ok," I replied.

"Hey, Norris, can I talk to you for a second," I asked, pulling him from his boys.

"Yeah, what's up? Y'all good?"

"Yeah, we're good. We are about to leave. I'll pick you up at noon tomorrow, so be ready."

"Ok, I'll be up. I can't let my princess down," he said to me, laughing and playing with Mani.

"I'm serious."

"I am too, I'll be up."

"Alright! Don't make me knock your door off the fuckin' hinge."

"So, you gon' be one of those crazy baby mamas, huh?" Norris joked.

"Ha ha, funny."

He gave baby girl a big hug, and then asked me if he could walk us out. The three of us walked out, and when I looked back to see if Gracie was behind us, I saw Steven, Rocko, Michelle and Chanel all lookin' at us. I smirked and kept walkin'.

When we got to the car, Norris tucked Armani in her car seat and gave her, her sippy cup. He walked over to me and started talking, telling me how he enjoyed having her there and how he wanted to come and spend more time with her. He wanted to start off slow because he knew I wouldn't allow him to take her to his place. Norris understood why and agreed that coming to my place made more sense. When we got to the end of our conversation, Gracie was walking up, so he told us bye. Gracie and I got in the car and left.

Chapter 18

"Expecting the Unexpected"

The day had finally come to find out the truth! We pulled up to Norris's spot at 11:45am. I told him I would be there at noon. I was a little early, so I was prepared to wait. I texted him twice, he didn't respond. I called him, he didn't answer. I sat in the car, and as time went on, I got angry. I hoped he wasn't standing us up, after being reminded the night before and agreeing to do it.

I kept calling, but he didn't answer. I honked the horn and looked at his windows, hoping he would peep out, but he didn't. I got so fed up, I took Mani out the car seat, walked up three damn flights of stairs and went to bam on his door. I wasn't leaving without his ass being in that car! I knocked almost 20 times before he answered. When he answered, he was in his underwear.

Apparently, he overslept because he got drunk last night. He was not ready and it was noon. Thankfully, we didn't have an appointment, we were just walk-in's, or else I would have strangled his ass. He welcomed us in to wait for him as he got ready. The place was neat and smelled good. It was cleaner than I thought it would be for a man who lived alone.

"There are some drinks in the fridge and snacks in the cabinet. Y'all are welcome to it. Give baby girl some snacks or something," he yelled to me from the bedroom.

I got up and walked in the kitchen, which was also kept up well. The fridge was stocked, and snacks were in almost all the cabinets. I was quite impressed.

While I snooped around his living room a little, my baby followed me. *A little investigator in training*, I thought. Mommy taught her all the secrets and gave her tips, as we walked around and looked in his shit. I was only looking for clues that he had a high traffic of women coming through. If that test showed he was the father, I would eventually allow him to bring my kid here. I needed to see how he was livin' and what type of environment my kid would be in. It was only right!

When he got in the shower, I wanted to go in his bedroom and look, but that was way too close to the bathroom. It was a huge possibility I could get caught. I would be so embarrassed, if I got caught snooping. I sat Mani on the chair, while she ate her chips. He didn't have a TV in the living room area. Trying not to overstep my boundaries too much, I tried asking him through the bathroom door if we could watch TV in his bedroom.

He couldn't hear me and told me to open the door and ask. When I opened the bathroom door, the steam filled the little room, but all I saw was dick. He had his dick sticking out the shower curtain, knowing I was going to open the bathroom door. A fucking setup... ok. It looked good, though. I wasn't going to fall for that. NOPE! When he told me it was ok, I closed the door and took my kid in the room to watch cartoons.

Mani and I sat in the room and waited for him. About three minutes after going in his room, she fell asleep. When I heard the shower turn off, I got up and went in the bathroom. After what I saw, I couldn't help myself. I went in and he was stepping out the shower. There I was, caught in action. I didn't want him to catch me walking in, I don't know why, but it felt awkward. I closed the toilet and sat on the seat, as he dried off.

He stood in front of me and I stroked his shit back and forth a little bit with my hands. He tried pushing my head toward it, but I told him quickly, "The dick ain't mine, so I'm not sucking it, but with protection, I'll fuck it." When I said that, he left out the bathroom, pullin' me, by the waist of my pants, behind him. He went in the room, saw Mani was sound asleep, and it was a wrap.

He took me in the living room, putting the condom on as we walked down the hall, and unbuckling my pants at the same time. By the time we got to the living room, I was naked. The apartment was so small, it all happened just that fast. Next thing I knew, I was bent over the couch, hair getting pulled, ass was clapping loudly, and I moaned, as if my life depended on it. He beat the pussy up.

I knew we were supposed to be on our way, but I didn't care about any of that. I was tempted to postpone for another day. The sex was so damn good, I didn't want to stop. I couldn't stop. I knew if I mentioned stopping, Norris would only go longer.

What the fuck am I doing? Why am I doing this? Oh shit, it feels so good! Don't stop, Norris! Quiet down, Tara, I said in my head. Before I knew it, I started speaking out.

"Yeah, Norris! Oh yeah! Right there! Keep going! Keep going! Harder! Don't stop." Then, came my orgasm.

I got wetter and he kept on going. He stopped to take one condom off and put on another; but when he did, it felt like he was still in, so I kept moaning. He shoved it back in and we went for, probably, another 15 minutes before stopping.

I wanted to go all day, but we had shit to do. I can't even lie; good dick will make a bitch get sidetracked. That was the first time I had fucked another guy while still being married. I felt like a damn slut. I felt horrible! I regretted it, just a little, but a part of me wished Chris walked in on us, so he could feel what I felt.

Wow! I couldn't believe I was still fucking the guy that broke my virginity years ago. Guess he couldn't get enough of this pussy, like I told him he wouldn't! Or was it me? Maybe I couldn't stay away from the dick. I don't know what it was. What I can say is, we made the best of it, every, single time we did it.

We finally arrived at our destination. Norris started getting out the car, until he saw that I was still sitting there. I was beyond nervous. As he tried to settle me, he kissed me on the lips, and said, "Baby, it's gon' be alright." He unbuckled my seat belt and told me to get out. The day seemed to get weirder as it went on.

We were in there for about an hour, and when we walked out, it felt good. We went on a Sunday, so they told us the results would take a little longer to come back. She gave me a paper with a website on it and my login and told me to go on the site to set up a password. I was told in three-four days to check the site to see the results. I was overly anxious to know what it said, it was going to be the longest three-four days of my life.

When I got in the car, I got a call. It was my realtor. He told me that there was a couple who made an offer on the house and they were ready to pay and sign papers. The house was in Both, me and Chris' name, so that meant I would have to talk to him about getting here to do all the paperwork as well. That was the part that sucked.

I dropped Norris off and went home. When I got home, I called Chris to let him know about the house and that I needed him to come back home to sign the papers with me. He didn't answer, as usual, so I left him a voicemail. The entire time I was trying to leave a voicemail, my phone started buzzing nonstop.

It was Gracie and Anthony. I called Gracie back. When I called her back, she was like," Listen! You know I hate to get in the middle of other people's drama, but you're my girl."

Dying to know what she needed to tell me, I was like, "What's going on, Gracie? Wassup?"

"Girl, you would not believe what I heard!"

"What? What? Tell me," I responded.

"Why I heard through the grapevine that Chris got a new girl?"

"He's a ho! I can believe it! Is it one of his employees, again?"

"No, girl! It's Chanel! Now, don't go off just yet! I still don't know if it's true. Like I said, it's a rumor!"

"Obviously, some shit had to pop off for anyone to get that impression of them two. She been on that funny shit, Gracie! My dumbass brushed it off, though, without getting to the bottom of it from the beginning. Hold on! Are you sure? She told me she was dealing with Andrew and they're always together."

"Listen, I'm just telling you what I heard!"

"I appreciate it!"

"Bye, girl, and don't do nothin' crazy!"

The rumor was not hard to believe at all. Chanel probably wanted Chris since the first time she saw him, but I wasn't sure if Chris would actually be into her. He knew how close we were. I don't think he would mess with her.

I called Chris, after hanging up with Gracie. Surprisingly, he picked up the first time. I was almost positive he didn't check his voicemail, so I told him that we had an offer on the house and the buyers were ready to sign. I asked him when he would be able to come and sign papers with me. He caught a huge attitude, as if we never spoke about selling the house before.

"I don't have time to do it! I don't want to sell the house anyways! You want the money, you find a way on your own, bitch!"

That started an argument. We argued and argued until I got so mad that I hung up. I couldn't believe it. Now, he had caused me to waste so many people's time, including my own. I couldn't sell the house without his signatures, so that left me no choice but to turn up a $190,000 offer.

It wasn't even about the money. I wanted the house off my hands. I didn't want anything to do with the house anymore, which was my purpose for moving out. Honestly, I wanted to get rid of everything we shared together. From the looks of it, Chris wasn't going to make it easy. He was really being a bitch to me, as if he wasn't the one who did wrong and tore our family apart from the beginning.

I knew it was him being bitter because I was happy! Before we had the fallout and I stormed out, leaving him looking like a damn fool, he was fine with everything. Now, he knew he couldn't get me back and I was moving on, he didn't want to help me. Either he wanted to keep a reason to stay in touch with me, or he really had that petty bitch in his ear, turning him against me.

I hadn't spoken to Anthony in a few days, so I picked up the phone to call him, only to see I already had over 20 missed calls and like seven text messages from him. I already told him that I was busy and dealing with a lot the last time I talked to him. I told him I would call him when I could, and he said he understood. It had me confused to why he had been calling and texting so much.

Then, I thought, maybe it's something serious because he hadn't done that lately, so I decided to call. I waited patiently, as the phone rang for him to pick up, but he didn't. I called, again, but still got no answer.

That wasn't like him. He picked up on the first ring almost every time I called him. It started to worry me. I sat in the car in front of the boutique and called four more times, but again, there was no answer. I texted him and he didn't respond. When we first started talking, I asked him where he lived, while I was in search for a new place. I didn't want to end up being his neighbor. As weird as it would be to pop up at his house, when I never wanted him to do it to me, I did.

He told me the neighborhood, but he didn't give me the exact address. I knew exactly where it was, and I was somewhat familiar with it, so I drove up and down the streets, looking for his car. I pulled on the last street left, and it was lit up with red, white and blue lights from fire trucks, ambulances and police cars.

As I rode down the street, I said to myself, "I sure hope whoever's injured is ok." It looked serious. I could hardly get down the street because so many cars and trucks were blocking the way. When I got half way down, I thought I saw Anthony's car, so I pulled over and walked down to the house where the car was. I prayed that if it was his house, everything was ok.

It seemed as if I was moving too slow. I ran down to the house with Armani in my arms. When I got close to the house, an officer stopped me and started asking questions. As we were talking to one another, I saw the coroner rolling out a body bag. Tears started rolling down my face. Seeing that made it difficult for me to speak. I was so concerned about whose body lied within, I struggled to answer the officer's questions.

I thought about what could have happened to Anthony. Damn, was he really dead? I wouldn't be able to answer any of his calls or texts anymore. He wouldn't be able to annoy me anymore. I was just starting to like him; now, he was gone. Too many funerals were happening back to back. People close to me were dropping like flies. I couldn't take it. I stood in the yard, sobbing heavily, and then Anthony walked out the house!

He was crying. I had never seen him so upset. I yelled his name, and he came over to me and told the officer it was fine, so they could stop bothering me.

"What happened?! I thought you were dead! My heart got heavy when I saw the body bag being rolled out. What happened," I asked, again.

"It's my grandma," he mourned.

"She's gone!" he continued!

Chapter 19

"Repairing a Broken Heart"

I stayed with Anthony at the house for a while. It was getting late and I had Mani with me, so I decided to head on home. He had his family and friends there, so I knew he would be fine, but I told him to call me if he needed me.

When I got home, I got us settled, tucked Mani in and went to bed. I was in a deep sleep, until I heard a knock on my door. They knocked and knocked and knocked. When I finally decided to get up, I looked at the clock on my nightstand and it read 3:47am. I couldn't help but wonder who the hell was at my door that time of morning.

So much shit was going on lately, I started to get nervous. I got up out my bed, slid on my slippers, grabbed my bat from beside my bed and headed to the door.

"Who is it," I asked, through the door.

The guy responded, "Me!"

I was still half sleep; my brain wasn't processing the voice. I looked through the peephole, but I couldn't really tell who it was.

My phone rung, so I ran back in the room to answer it. It was Anthony, telling me he was at the door. I knew he just had death in his family and I was there comforting him, but damn, that didn't mean I was ok with being a booty call tonight. I opened the door, with a slight attitude. I felt bad for the guy, so I didn't want to come off too harsh, but I did get straight to the point.

I opened the door, and as he walked in, looking at the bat in my hand. I said, "Hey, I'm shocked to see you at 4a.m with no prior calls."

"I called, Tara. I called multiple times, but you didn't answer."

I looked at my phone and there it was, six missed calls from Anthony. I felt like an idiot.

"I came on by anyway because you didn't answer. I hope it's ok. I couldn't sleep in the house alone, after what just happened tonight. I needed some company, but I preferred yours. Is it ok I crash here?"

"Oh no, no problem! Make yourself at home. I totally understand."

I was so embarrassed by how I acted towards him and how I looked. I was in the worst clothes ever, I had morning breath, eye boogers in my eyes, even dried drool on the side of my face. I couldn't believe how I looked in front of him.

He told me he would sleep on the couch. I gave him a pillow and a blanket and told him I'd be in my room if he needed me. I went in my room and closed my bedroom door. I got in the bed and stared at the ceiling.

I laid there in guilt about making him sleep on that uncomfortable couch. I knew for sure he would wake up with a stiff neck in the morning. We were just friends and all, but I wanted to invite him in the bed with me. I wasn't tryin' to fuck him or anything. I wondered if he would try me if I did tell him to come in, though. As I was laying down, thinkin' about all this, I got a knock on my room door.

"Come in," I yelled.

"Do you mind if I grab a glass of wine out the fridge?"

"No, go right ahead. I'll take a glass too, actually."

He went in the kitchen, fixed the wine and brought it to me. I was going to be up for a few hours, so why not drink a glass of wine? After he handed me the wine, he started to leave out the room, but I told him he could stay, if he wanted, and I could find a movie for us to watch.

We ended up watching one of my favorite movies that turned out to be one of his favorites as well, *Ride Along*. It was a comedy, so we sat up in the bed, laughing hysterically, as we sipped our wine. Kevin Hart was a damn fool.

He told me how much he appreciated me opening my place to him and being there for him. Just a few years ago, I felt the same way he did, so it was nice to be that person for him. It was also great to feel appreciated - for once.

By the time the movie went off, he was sound asleep in the bed. I took the glass out his hand, sat it on the nightstand and tucked him underneath the covers. I got in the bed, on the opposite side, turned my back to him and went to sleep.

When we woke up the next morning, he was laying behind me, with his arms over me, holding me close to him. As I woke up, I felt hard dick on my ass. Still half asleep, I started grinding on it. Waking up, being held tightly with hard dick on me felt good as hell. I hadn't had that in a long time. It was so comforting, and it always made me feel at peace. Well, almost always, until I realized who was holding me.

It wasn't so much that it was Anthony, but we had never gotten that close before. I didn't know what he was workin' with and I wasn't trying to find out anytime soon. I wanted to take things slowly, but it was too late for that! Although I wanted to try him badly, I'd been holdin' back for quite some time.

I jumped up, waking him out his sleep. Not only was he laying behind me with his shit pokin' on my ass, he had somehow come out of his clothes and was in his boxers only, which didn't help much, because his dick was hanging out. As I jumped out the bed, I threw the covers back. I threw it so far back, I saw everything.

It was all right there, so... shit, I looked. It was lying peacefully on my silk sheets.

"What are you doing?" I yelled.

"What, Tara? What's wrong?"

I looked down and pointed.

"Oh, that! I'm sorry, I didn't mean to do any of this. I'm sorry," he said, as he got out the bed, stuffing it all in his boxer briefs.

"I didn't mean to sleep in here. I actually wanted to sleep on the couch because I didn't want to make you uncomfortable. Somehow, in my sleep, I slipped off the rest of my clothes. I'm so sorry, Tara."

I told him it was ok, it was unexpected, all of that, (if you know what I mean). He wasn't the best. His shit wasn't as big as I was used to, but I could manage. He wasn't as disappointing as that white chocolate I had back in college, though, I can tell you that. I was scared to fuck with light-skinned niggas after him. That shit was about the size of a Vienna sausage, I kid you not, but Anthony was ok.

He was something serious. He looked damn good lying in my bed too. While admiring Anthony's fine-ass, Armani started crying. She was right on time to break the awkwardness.

Four days went by and it was time to view his grandmother's body. I went with him for support, and afterwards, we all went to Anthony's house for the gathering and dinner. I told him I wouldn't stay the entire time and that I had to go get Mani and head home. He said ok and asked if he could come back over. I told him it was ok and to call when he was on his way.

When I got home, I made dinner. I was acting cute around his family, so I picked over my food and hardly ate. I didn't go all out for dinner. I kept it simple; yellow rice, baked chicken and steamed broccoli. When I was done with dinner, baby girl and I ate, and then I washed her and put her to bed. It was maybe 11pm when I was done with all that, so I got in the shower. Soon as I stepped in the shower, my phone rang. I started to let it ring, but I thought maybe it was Anthony.

I got out the shower, looked at my phone, and sure enough, it was. He told me he was outside the door. "Oh shit! I'm naked." My body was slightly wet, so I couldn't just throw on clothes. I ran in the bathroom, almost busted my ass, and I grabbed a towel and wrapped it around me.

I went to the door and opened it.

"You called as soon as I got in the shower. I'm just going to finish washing and I'll be right out."

He said, "Ok."

I noticed he had a duffle bag in his hand, but I was worried about being naked, so I didn't acknowledge that.

When I got out, I got dressed. I threw on one of those nightgowns and went out to the living room where Anthony was. I never wore a bra or underwear to bed, so I didn't have any on. When I walked out, I told him he could go in the shower when he was ready. I went in the kitchen and fixed some wine, as my ass jiggled around in the nightgown. When I turned around, Anthony was all over me, looking as if he had never seen ass before.

"It smells good in here! What did you cook," he asked me, as he walked in the kitchen.

I showed him what was on the stove.

"Want some?" I asked.

"Some of what?"

"Food, silly," I said, blushing.

"Hell yeah! If you don't mind fixing it."

"I got you!"

"Do you want some wine too," I asked.

"No, I'm good. I had some liquor."

I didn't know he drunk alcohol. Curious to know what he was drinking, I asked. He told me he had Crown Apple with no chaser. Once he said that, I gave him the side-eye. See, I knew how these niggas were once they drank, especially off brown liquor. After seeing how Chris acted drunk, I was very cautious around drinking men. I was alone too. No way in hell I was fuckin' with a nigga like Chris again. That was my first time and my last.

He sat on the couch, eating and I sat on the other couch, sippin' my wine.

"So, do you drink often," I asked.

"Oh no, only when I'm really stressed, to be honest."

"Oh...ok. That's good to know!"

"Dealing with everything today drove me to the bottle."

"I get it, but you can't handle situations like that! That's how people become alcoholics.

"I know," he told me, putting his head down in shame.

I got up from the couch, carrying his plate in the kitchen, and told him, "Let me get you a towel and washcloth."

I went in the bathroom and sat it on the counter next to the sink. When I was walking out the bathroom, he was walking in. I started to walk around him, but he grabbed me by the waist. He told me to look at him. I stood in front of him and looked up into his beautiful-ass eyes.

"I appreciate you, sweetie. I want you to know that," he told me.

I looked at him and told him it wasn't a problem. Then, he rested his head on top of mine and moved his hands on my butt.

"I've never had a woman like you in my life. I wanted you badly, and now that I got you, I want you to know I would never fuck this up. I put that on my grandma."

He loved the hell out of his grandma, with all his heart, so when he told me that, I knew it was real. Especially, when I felt tears drop on my forehead.

I wiped his tears and told him, "Go 'head in the shower, I'll be right here when you get out."

I sat on the bed, watching The Real Housewives of Atlanta, as I normally did on a Sunday night. When he got out the shower, he had a towel wrapped around him. He looked damn good. I wanted to eat his fine-ass up.

When he walked out of the room, into the living room, he came back in his briefs. He put the towel in the dirty clothes hamper and came and laid across the bed. He watched my show with me, and then came and hugged up on me. I didn't resist either. He smelled good, felt good and looked good! They say good things don't last forever. So, I might as well enjoy it while I could.

I got out the bed and went to pee, and when I came back in the room, he was in the middle of the bed and told me to come sit on daddy. I had no panties on. I didn't know if I was ready. That side of Anthony turned me on. Normally, he would be shy and limited to the things he said because he didn't want to overstep any boundaries, but that night, he was loose and didn't give a fuck. I didn't know if he was loosening up to me, or if the liquor was to blame.

I told him I didn't know if it was a good idea and he asked me why. I lifted my nightgown and showed him. Then, he said, "Even better." From that point, I knew what type of night it would be.

I got on the bed and I sat on Anthony. I hated when a nigga called themselves daddy. I always felt that wasn't a title that was given, but earned. When I sat on Anthony, my juices soaked his briefs, instantly. He couldn't believe it, so he lifted me up a little bit and put his hand down there. He rubbed me to see if it was what he thought it was and I could feel him getting excited. It never took long for me to get wet for a nigga I wanted.

Within a minute, he was completely hard, and he was sliding on a condom. I'd started something I never wanted to finish. By the end of the night, I was calling him daddy and called him that every moment after. He gave me the ride of my life. They say, "It ain't 'bout what you got, it's how you use it," and that damn sure was the truth. His shit wasn't the biggest, but the way he fucked me made up for that. None of that was supposed to happen, but I knew what it was like trying to heal a hurting heart.

Chapter 20

"Calling it Quits"

Next morning, I'm lying in the bed next to Daddy, feeling like a new woman. He was lying behind me, again, holding me, but this time felt better than the last and I didn't want to move. The night before was amazing. I thought I was whipped. Before that, I wanted to just be friends, but after what went down, I didn't want him to have anyone else. He was mine and didn't know it. We were still friends, but I was the only friend he was allowed to have. He turned me into this psychotic bitch I never thought a light-skinned nigga could make me.

I'm lying in the bed with Daddy and I hear the doorbell ring. Daddy looked at me and I looked at him. He could tell I wasn't expecting anyone, so he told me to stay in bed and that he would get it, so I listened. He could tell me to do anything and I would do it.

He answered the door and told me I had a package to sign for. I wasn't expecting any packages. I thought maybe Chris came to his senses and sent Mani some clothes or something. Then, I remembered, he didn't know where I lived to have my address. It was strange. I'm thinking about all of this, as I got dressed.

When I got to the door, I greeted the delivery guy with a smile and a good morning. I had an amazing night, so I was up early, feeling great! He asked me if I was Tara Anderson and I told him yes, I was. I was still smiling. Then, he told me I had to sign before receiving my package. Ok, cool. No problem. Then, he handed me a big envelope and told me, "Tara Anderson, you have been served," and he ran off.

Daddy and I was still standing in the door, looking at each other. Served with what? I didn't do shit to anybody to be getting served anything. What the hell was this? I had never gotten anything like it before. Daddy closed and locked the door, as I was opening the envelope. He was standing right beside me, while I pulled the papers out. Chris had filed for divorce.

We were separated a while and hadn't talked in months. Daddy was making me happy and I wanted him, but to see and hold those papers in my hand was a different story. I was speechless. I still loved Chris. Daddy asked me, "What's wrong? What is it," but I couldn't speak.

He slid the papers out my hand and read them. He put it on the counter for me. He took me to the couch, sat me down and hugged me. I knew he would be happy to know that this was happening, and I was too, but a part of me was sad, for some reason. I knew we weren't going to be together, but a divorce was the last thing I expected. I'd trained my mind to think that I was moving on and doing better, but in reality, I wasn't.

I started to think, maybe this is the best for us, especially me. Soon, I would be able to do what I want as a free woman, but here I was, not even 30 yet, getting a divorce. I'd just heard he was messing around with Chanel, so I couldn't help but wonder if she was the reason behind all of that. Was this payback from her getting served with papers?

It was one thing after another. I was already paying a lawyer to help me with the case I had with Chanel. Now, I needed another attorney for the divorce. It was all crazy to me. Seemed like every time I started to enjoy life and tried to be happy, something or someone came along and took my joy.

Daddy got dressed and told me he was heading out. He wanted to give me some space and told me to call him if I needed him. I was happy he did that. I needed that time to really process what just happened. I wanted to call Chris but didn't know if it would be a bad idea, so I didn't. Instead, I called Gracie.

"Hey, girl," I said to her.

"Hey! I haven't heard from you in a while. Anthony must have you boo'd up these days?"

I started smiling. "Yeah, we've been kickin' it lately. You know his grandma passed away recently, so he was over with me and Mani because he didn't want to stay at his place. I must say, it's been nice havin' him around. I called you about something else, though."

"What's going on, Tara?"

"I got served with divorce papers this morning."

"I didn't know y'all were to that point. What made him do this?"

"I didn't know either. I was in disbelief. To be quite honest with you, I think Chanel may have been in his ear about this."

"So, you know for sure they're dealin'?"

"No, but I have a feeling."

"Well, have you tried reaching out to him?"

"I didn't know if I should."

"I don't see any harm in it. Just watch what you say. Divorces can get really tricky, so just be careful You never know who is watching and will testify against you with the divorce and the Chanel case.

"Thanks, girl."

"No problem; let me know if I can help."

When I hung up from Gracie, I called Chris. The first time, he didn't answer. I waited about 25 minutes and called again.

"Hello?!"

"Hey... I got served with the papers today. Didn't know you was even thinking about this."

"Well, things happen. Last time we spoke, it didn't sound like we would ever get back together, so we might as well move on."

"Yeah, you're absolutely right. I just want you to know I appreciate this, and I'll see you in court."

"See you there," he said, and then we hung up.

I immediately started looking for an attorney to back me up with this divorce. I found a couple, but there was one in particular I wanted to meet with. She told me she was available to meet, so I got dressed. I was going to drop Mani off to the babysitter, but then Josh and Gracie wanted her, so I dropped her off to them for a while.

When I went to pick Mani up from Josh and Gracie's crib, I stayed for a little while, talking and laughing with them. Gracie told me she wanted to go back home for a day to visit her family, but she didn't want to fly alone. The only problem was she didn't have anyone to go with her. Josh had to work, so I told her I would go with her, not knowing it was for the next day until after I had already agreed to it.

I had this manager at the shop for a while who was doing amazing. She was promoted from sales associate when Michelle left. Mani's sitter was able to take care of her the entire day I would be gone. Anthony had a key to my place, so he could get in. I had everything under control, everything was taken care of. I was ready to take the trip.

On my way to Atlanta, I thought about popping up to Chris' house. I wondered if he would be at the club for me to do some snooping. I was curious to see what I could find. He didn't know I would be in the "A," so that would be perfect.

When we landed, I was going to get a hotel, but Gracie insisted on me staying at her mom's house, so I did. Before I went there, Gracie and I made a stop. When I rode pass Chris' house, his car was gone. So, I swung by the club to be sure he was working and not running a quick errand. Sure enough, his car was there. Since he was at work, I knew I had some time, so I went back to the house to see if my key still worked.

When I went to the door, put my key in and turned the knob, it unlocked, so we proceeded to go in. Gracie was so nervous. It wasn't like what we were doing was illegal because, technically, it was still my house too. When we went in, we were laughing and giggling loudly, as we went up the stairs. When I went in the bedroom, Chanel was standing in the middle of the floor in lingerie.

Gracie's mouth dropped. I wasn't expecting to see her either. It felt like déjà vu when he had that other bitch in the house and I caught them fucking. I had heard the rumors about Chanel and Chris, and I even asked him if there was someone else. He lied.

I didn't get mad that time. For some odd reason, I couldn't. Instead, I pulled my phone out and started taking pictures. I told Gracie to record as well. Chanel started to get mad. She started cursing and even wanted to fight me. She was hyped and ready to throw down, until I put her in her place.

I reminded her that I was still legally his wife and owner of that house, and how I had the authority and say so to have her removed by force. She knew it was true, although she didn't want to be reminded of it, and calmed down quickly. She was still talking her shit, walking around the house, as if she owned the place.

From the looks of it, it looked like he even moved her in. She was comfortable as hell. Chanel was walking around in lingerie, dinner was cooked on the stove, and the table was set romantically. There was no way in hell I was gonna be a fool and believe they'd just started dealing. The shit she was doing seemed like they'd been fucking for months.

I walked around, looking and taking pictures, as Gracie followed me with the video. My best friend, who I once looked at and loved as a sister, was now fucking the man I was still married to. No matter how much I tried brushing it off, I couldn't ignore the situation. Even though Chris and I was done and me and Chanel's friendship had fallen apart, it still hurt me to know that they both would do me so dirty.

When I was looking through the house, Chanel decided to call Chris. I didn't know which Chris I would get, and I had my seven-month pregnant friend with me, so I decided to leave before he got there. I got more than what I came for, so I was happy. By the time Chris got there, we were already gone. I promised Josh to keep her and the baby safe, as he did with my baby girl.

Chris called me. He blew my phone up, but I didn't answer. Enough lies were told to me. He stood in that house crying. He told me he'd never messed with anybody else. All along it was a lie. For God knows how long, they were having an affair. For all I knew, he could have been messing around with her before her and I fell out.

Chapter 21

"Facing the Truth"

When I came back home, Anthony was still in bed asleep. I didn't tell him about the adventure I had in Atlanta. It was crazier than I expected. When he woke up, I did tell him a little bit, though. I told him how I found out my best friend was really sleepin' with my husband.

I forgot all about the DNA results, with all the shit that was going on. That was one hell of a week. So much was being revealed to me, forcing me to face the truth that I wasn't ready to deal with.

Everything was all coming together. As I sat in the living room, I played back everything in my head. From the time when Chanel made those slick comments about Chris in my room… To her always wanting to be around us... Even the time when I gave her time off from the boutique to go to Atlanta. I was such a dummy. I played myself. I couldn't believe the level of betrayal they were on.

I didn't know if their relationship was genuine or if he was using Chanel to get back at Norris. I didn't know if Chanel was using Chris to get back at me. It was one, big circle full of *LOVE, LIES* and *BETRAYAL*. It was all coming to me now. It even made me think that no one around me would ever be as loyal to me as I was to them. It started to fuck with my head.

I slid off the couch onto the floor. My body got weak. My mouth watered, and I began to feel nauseous. I couldn't believe what was happening. I got up off the floor, as quickly as I could, and ran in the bathroom. I started vomiting. It came up and I couldn't hold back.

Daddy came to check on me. He was concerned. I told him I couldn't handle life anymore. It was getting to be too much for me. I had taken all I could take. I didn't want to deal with anyone else or the bullshit that came with them.

He looked at me, with tears in his eyes.

"Tara? Baby? What are you saying?"

"I...I can't do this anymore!"

"Do what, Tara?"

"Life, Anthony! Life! It's too much for me!"

I snatched my arms away from him and ran in the kitchen.

He followed behind me. I went in the drawer and I grabbed a knife, ready to slit my wrist. He grabbed the knife, trying to stop me.

He held it and he whispered to me, "I can't lose you! I can't lose anybody else! You are perfect. You are my everything. I don't know what I would do without you. Please, baby, give me the knife, let it go. Please, baby...just give it to me. That little girl needs you! I need you!"

Tears started rolling down my checks, as my mascara went along with it. I had never been suicidal in my life. I've always loved living and made the best of every day. With everything going on around me, I was losing my mind, literally. Why me?

I had never dealt with mental illness. I never really thought depression was real, but something wasn't right with me. I stood in the kitchen with my feet in between life and death, ready to take my own life, because of the pain others had caused me. I realized no matter what you have or how happy you think you are, there is no tricking your mind into believing something that isn't real.

Thankfully, I had someone on my side who really cared about me and my kid. Without him being there, I probably would have been dead because of my own selfishness. I wasn't even thinking about my daughter and what life would bring to her if I left her behind with someone else. I wanted to give up completely, until I came to some of my senses, and looked up on the wall at my daughter's picture.

"I can't do this, I cried. It's not fair to her, to me, to you," I told Anthony.

"I gotta stay strong! I gotta push through! The devil won't defeat me! That little girl needs me! I have to be here for her," I repeated, to myself.

Anthony just stood there, looking and listening to me. I was sure he wanted nothing to do with me anymore. He probably thought I was a crazy bitch. He probably didn't want to sleep under the same roof as me again.

Trying to clear my mind off things, Daddy reminded me about the thing I needed to do on my phone. He didn't know what it was, exactly, because I never told him. When I went to get my phone out the bedroom, I told Daddy to sit next to me. At that moment, I told him what it was. I told him the entire situation and that I was taking the next step for my daughter. I started to login, but then I stopped. I handed the phone to Daddy and told him to click the button. When he started to click it, I snatched the phone back and told him never mind.

Then, he looked at me and said, "Either you're going to do it this time, or I will! We are not going to do this all day."

So, I did the honors and clicked it, but I handed the phone to him for him to read the results. I wished neither Chris or Norris could be the father, to be honest. I didn't want Chanel to be my daughter's aunt or stepmom and I didn't want any ties to Chris after the divorce; but unfortunately, one of them was. I just didn't want those type of problems. Then, daddy read the results.

The test showed that Norris was 99.99% the father. I almost had another breakdown. I couldn't believe what I heard. I didn't care about Chris' feelings at all, because he never cared about my kid anyway. Daddy handed me the phone for me to see for myself. I threw the phone down.

"Now what," Daddy asked me.

"Well, I don't know! It is what it is. I can't change any of this," I told him.

"Have you spoken to any of them lately?"

"Well, when Norris and I went to do the test, he acted as if he would be fully involved if he was the father. Chris, on the other hand, don't know we went to do the test. With the whole divorce thing going on, I don't know when a good time is to speak on it," I told him.

"Well, at least you know for sure. You all deserve that. Even Chris! At least once the divorce is over, you don't have to deal with him anymore," Daddy said.

"Yeah, I know, but regardless of that, Chanel will still be in my life. That's Norris' sister and Mani's... Mani's aunt," I said, hesitantly.

"Oh," Daddy said, with a long face.

"I just want you to know I'll be here with you every step of the way," he told me, hugging me and kissing me on the forehead.

After reading the results, I called the divorce lawyer. I asked for her guidance on how, and if, I should mention this to Chris. She told me to come on in and sit down with her, so we could talk about it. A few hours later, I went over to her office.

When I left out the lawyer's office, I sat in the car, contemplating what I would send to Chris, letting him know he wasn't Mani's father.

I just sent him a text saying, "After this divorce, you won't have to worry about me or Mani! I hope you got what you wanted."

He texted back, almost immediately, and the text read, "What's that supposed to mean?"

I sent a final text saying, "Whatever you want it to mean!"

He never responded back and neither did I.

I was sure once Norris found out he would end up telling Chanel and it would get back to Chris. I didn't care, though. I called Norris right after I finished texting Chris. I asked him if he had some time to talk. He told me to swing by and we could chat. I went by, as soon as I left the office.

He came outside, and we sat in the car.

"So, I got the results back from the test," I told Norris.

"Where's it at? What did it say?"

I said, "Well," and handed him my phone. He was so excited. More excited than I expected him to be.

"We both knew it, though," he said to me.

"Yeah, I guess we did," I told Norris.

"What's the matter? Are you not happy? I told you I would help and be the best I can be! What more do you want," Norris asked me.

"It's not you, Norris, I got a lot going on; and another thing, I don't want to deal with Chanel. Chris filed for divorce and I found out him and Chanel are messing around. I'm already taking her to court and I don't trust her around my kid," I told him.

He looked at me crazy. Apparently, he didn't know any of that. He hadn't heard from her in a while, he said. He also mentioned that she wasn't acting like herself lately. He offered to come to the house and take care of Mani while I got some things done or even got some rest. I told him I appreciated it and I would let him know. He handed me the money he had in his pocket, which was a little over $500, and told me to go shopping for her and he would get her some things as well.

I didn't know if I should take it. That was another issue I was concerned about. Norris was still in the streets and it scared me for me or my daughter to be around him. I knew he wouldn't put us in harm's way, but you just never knew what would happen. I've never dealt with street niggas, but Chanel did in the past. All I knew was the streets was wicked and I wanted no part in it.

When I got home, daddy was there. He told me he wanted to talk to me about something. I thought to myself, *please, no more bad news or drama!* I asked him what it was he wanted to talk about, and he told me his house. He told me he wanted to sell it.

He asked me if he could stay with me until he found another place, promising to meet me half way with bills, cleaning and cooking. It was cool with me. Armani and I loved having him there anyway.

Chapter 22

"Bittersweet"

Weeks went by and it was almost time for us to welcome baby Gracelyn Joniyah. That's right, it was a girl! They were celebrating with a beautiful baby shower. The theme was Twinkle, Twinkle Little Star. A decorator was hired and went over the top to make the place beautiful, the food was catered by one of Charlotte's finest and best soul food restaurants, tons of games were planned and lots of people were invited. Like Chanel always said, 'this bitch is bougie.' I was excited about this and there was no doubt about it. I was definitely in the building.

I wasn't looking forward to seeing Chris, though. If he even showed up. He was not only acting funny with me, lately, but with his family as well. If he came, I knew Chanel would be with him. Norris would be in the building for sure. Him and Josh are best friends. He wouldn't be missing this moment, unless he had gotten himself in some more shit again. I was prepared for a chaotic day. That's the price you paid when people you no longer dealt with was mutual friends with the people you fucked with. No matter what, there was no way of completely getting rid of them.

I didn't have a chance to tell Gracie the DNA results. Josh didn't mention anything about it to me either. He didn't say anything to me, so I figured he didn't know. Josh was really cool, though. I'm sure once he found out, he wouldn't look at me, love or treat Mani differently. He never judged anybody about shit they had going on; instead, he always offered help and support and that was one reason I fucked with him.

So, Gracie's family was coming from Atlanta for the shower. All our friends would be there. Well… Gracie's friends. I wasn't sure if I would see Michelle or not, but I didn't care. She didn't speak at the funeral, so I didn't expect her to speak at the shower.

We were having a ball. The place was packed. Gracie and Josh knew lots of people that came out and supported them. It was an amazing turnout. The room was filled with love, laughter and positivity. This was the energy I needed around me. I had gone through hell the past couple of weeks.

Daddy told me he didn't want to come because he didn't want to be around Norris and Chris, but I begged and convinced him to come. He finally agreed to it and told me he would meet me there. I gave him the address and told him to call me once he was outside, so I could come out and we could walk back in together.

I knew the feeling of walking into a room full of people you barely knew. He was shy around people he didn't know. I didn't want to run him off or have him feel uncomfortable, because I wanted him to stay with me the entire night.

I was hosting the baby shower, along with Gracie's sister-in-law. Gracie knew how silly we were, so we did what we had to do to make sure they had the best baby shower they could imagine. Gracie and Josh didn't have to spend a dime. Showing my appreciation for their loyalty, I funded the majority of the shower, with help from her parents. That was the least I could do. They'd been there for me through almost everything.

Josh and Chris's entire family was there. Their mom spoke to me, but not as much. I always felt like she didn't like me, but we were getting a divorce, so I was the last bitch she would ever have to worry about. I didn't like her ass either, so the feeling was mutual.

I continued to have fun and I tried my hardest to ignore the negativity. Gracie and I laughed and ate. Everything was going well. Everybody was having fun. I was enjoying myself so much, I almost forgot I was hosting. I was happy as hell I didn't run into Chris, until he showed up two hours into the baby shower.

He kept looking at me and it seemed like every time I looked around, we made eye contact. He never spoke to me, and I ignored him. When Gracie saw him, she came over to me and checked on me. I told her I would be ok. As soon as I told Gracie I was shocked he didn't bring his bitch, she walked in.

She looked like money. She must have been fuckin' with lots of husbands in Atlanta to get what she had. When she told me that she would be on top, I started to wonder if that meant on other women's men. Ha, she was an undercover slut. I should have kept my eyes on her. That was my first time seeing them together for myself. I can't even lie, I was a little annoyed and embarrassed, but I held my composure and didn't show emotions. She didn't speak either. Not that I expected her to. I ignored her, just as much as I ignored her dude. The way she acted while hearing my voice all night, it seemed like she was more upset with me than I was with her. From the look on her face, she was clearly bothered.

I knew she was on some petty shit, showing up with Chris in front of everybody. She was probably trying to make me jealous, but all she did was make herself look like a fool. Everybody knew she was my best friend. Everybody knew that was my husband, and now they were together. It wasn't a good look for either of them. Little did they know, I had a little secret of my own. I couldn't wait to see their faces once they saw what I'd been up to.

Thirty minutes later, Anthony called me and told me he was outside. When I went outside, he looked finer than he ever had. He went to the barbershop earlier, he was dressed nicely, he smelled good and just looked fine as hell - as usual. He always had swag, I never had to worry about that when it came to him. To say he was a Dominican, he outdid a lot of these niggas.

When we walked back in together, it seemed like everyone was lookin' at us. I introduced him to everyone at the shower as my friend. I wanted to tell them he was my boo, but we weren't official yet. That was the first time I was showing him off. I was there with my new boo, Chris was there with his bum, so everybody got the memo. He ended up chillin' with Josh, most of the night. We threw a couple shots back together and I got him to play games he was cool with. It seemed like he was loosening up and enjoying himself. It was a baby shower but felt more like a party.

Josh came to me and told me he liked Anthony. He told me he was a really cool guy, and how he knew some of Anthony's peoples. Anthony chilled with him for a while, until Chris came over. Daddy wasn't with no funny shit. He didn't care for Chris and damn sure wasn't gonna act like he did. He wasn't into fighting or arguing, but he also didn't play about me either. If he had to, he would. He knew what I went through with Chris. He already didn't care for him because of how he treated me, but he tried keeping the peace. Every time Chris was near, Daddy walked the opposite way.

As I'm hosting, I saw Allie and Gina walk in. I didn't have an issue with Allie or Gina, but they were Michelle's friends. Michelle didn't fuck with me, so I guess her posse didn't either. Hate by association, as they call it.

They saw me and rolled their eyes. I laughed and kept hosting. That eye-rolling shit was childish as fuck. I wanted one of them to step, so I could lay their asses out. I was having fun still, despite the demons that entered the room.

As I walked around, Josh pulled me to the side. He told me how he had a surprise for Gracie and needed my help. He told me to make sure Gracie's sister-in-law, Heather, was on board as well. I told him I would make sure of that.

Shorty after, Josh came to me. It was time to present the surprise to Gracie and the guests. We rounded everyone and had them all come in. As hard as it was, we asked everyone to get quiet. Josh spoke in the mic and faced Gracie. He poured his heart out to her and then got down on one knee. He continued to tell Gracie how he felt about her, in front of all their family and friends, as he opened a little box which held a beautiful, 14k, white gold, 3 carat, diamond ring.

He asked her to be his wife and she said yes. I was in tears, in fact, I think everyone was, even the guys. I looked over to my right and there Daddy was. Somehow, he'd made his way back to me and I didn't even know it. When I looked to the left, Chanel was next to Chris with her arm wrapped around him, as he stared at me.

A baby shower we were gathered for ended as an engagement party. Heather and I wasn't prepared, but at the parents-to-be/newly engaged couple's request, we did our best. The night was beautiful. Everything that happened was phenomenal, despite the shit I saw with my own eyes and some of the occupants that filled the room.

As the night started to wind down, I realized I didn't see Michelle or Norris. They were the only two missing in action. Norris almost never missed a gathering and Michelle's girls were here, so it was strange that she wasn't around. Not giving a fuck about their absence, I started drinking and dancing, you know, having a nice time. Thirty minutes after I mentioned it to Gracie, she tapped me on the shoulder and told me to look over by the door. Who was walking in the room together? Michelle and Norris. My sister and baby daddy were all hugged up...

About the Author

Courtney was born and raised in North Charleston, South Carolina, most of her life. She currently resides in a small town outside of North Charleston called Goose Creek, with her son and daughter.

Although she has an Associate's in Health Science and has been in healthcare most of her career, her passion for writing lead her to chase her dreams. Courtney has always been thrilled to write and use her imagination, and she has been writing short stories since a young age. As she grew older and experienced more of life, writing became more than just a hobby; she found it therapeutic. As she wrote more, she knew she wanted to be a published author. Courtney has so many stories to tell!

When she isn't reading or turning her imagination into a work of art, she is spending time with her family, in front of a camera, or watching shows she loves, such as *Power*, *Saints and Sinners*, *Hell's Kitchen* and *The Chi*.

With the links below, you can connect with Courtney for upcoming events, appearances, to purchase books, or simply to give her feedback at:

Instagram: @authorcourtneysimone

Facebook: @officialcourtneysimone

Website: www.dreaminkpub.com For business inquires: contactcourtneys@gmail.com

www.ingramcontent.com/pod-product-compliance
Lightning Source LLC
Chambersburg PA
CBHW060930180626
46817CB00004B/1479